Inner Heart`s Calling

Copyright © October 2020
Dina Santosh

ISBN 9798550333051
The moral right of the author has been asserted.
All rights reserved

All characters appearing in this book are fictional and any resemblance to real persons, living or dead are purely coincidental

Dedication:

I would like to thank my family for their unstinting support in the writing of this book and all the teachers who have come my way. Special thanks to Marilyn Alauria who has given me the courage to bring this book to fruition.

Chapter 1

"Promise me you will deliver this to the address on the envelope…no matter what" whispered the stranger as he lay injured from a wound to his side, surreptitiously trying to thrust an envelope into her hand with an address which she barely had time to read.

Without giving it a second glance she stuffed it deep into the inside pocket of her cardigan underneath the tissues she had there making sure it would not fall out accidentally giving her the opportunity to inspect it later on.

Please don`t tell anyone though, or your life will be in danger", he added, as he grabbed her hand.

He was now holding on to it so tightly that she wanted to pull it away immediately to set herself free from this stranger but she couldn`t as his grip became stronger and his hand closed around hers, to make sure that she could not get away from him.

For someone who was bleeding so profusely his strength was not fading at all, in fact, his grip was still very powerful and she felt as though her hand was slowly being strangled as her fingers folded tightly inside each other in his grip. Her hand was squashed and it became really uncomfortable as the flow of blood started to drain away from her arm, the circulation becoming so reduced that it restricted her movement and it felt like a rubber band slowly tightening and strangling her so that the inevitable pins and needles began to course through it and take over. As she looked down at her hand she could see them slowly swelling and beginning to go a pale blue colour and she tried to snatch it away from him to get the blood flowing back but his grip tightened even more as he pulled her closer to him and his next words made her draw breath and sent a chill down her spine at the same time. Through clenched teeth he whispered to her "they WILL kill you if they see you talking to me so go now, run and don`t look back…." The words were a whisper and she was unsure if she had heard them correctly as she strained closer but she was suddenly alert, her senses becoming heightened as he continued "Go, I promise this isn`t as serious as it looks" as he pointed to his wound. He loosened his grip and released her hand, so that she was finally relieved when she started feeling the blood flow back into her veins again but she did not feel comfortable leaving him alone and in such a state. Her other hand was placed on top of his stomach area where he had been wounded to put pressure on it to stem the flow of blood.

To any observer it looked as though she was comforting him and reassuring him that he would survive from this severe injury that appeared to be life-threatening.

He then whispered something unintelligible to her and tried to push her away from him to persuade her to go but she was having none of it as she was determined to be by his side until help arrived.

She was unsure that she had heard the stranger correctly and she continued to reassure him whilst she waited for the emergency services. A sense of panic was beginning to rise to the surface as blood started to gush out of his wound and she could no longer control the amount of blood escaping from the open gash, which seemed to be getting bigger and bigger. The seconds were passing really slowly and it felt to her as though everything was moving in slow motion. Even her vision was becoming blurred as she could only see herself and the stranger. It was as though she and he were the only person in the world at this moment and there was the feeling that only she could help him.

She felt as though his life depended on her next action and that thought brought on an even deeper sense of panic for if she left him as he had beseeched her to he would undoubtedly bleed to death and there was no-one to call on for assistance, just when she needed it the most.

She had recalled some of the her previous training from a First Aid course and taken action to exert some heavy pressure directly on his wound and used part of his clothing to help stem the blood flow with his hand now pressed tightly underneath hers.

"Hold on" she screamed "I can hear the ambulance, it`s just coming" she added as she heard the sirens fast approaching. She thought there were two different sounds but the noise was from a distance and she could have been mistaken, but as the sounds came closer she could hear alternate sirens and she thought that perhaps two ambulances had been called after all.

Her heart was pounding uncontrollably fast and it felt as though it may suddenly thrust out of her skin any moment and explode out of her body. She was praying for that ambulance to come quickly and deal with this situation because she felt she was out of her depth and although she had been on a First Aid course a few months earlier she was not prepared to deal with this type of injury and she vaguely remembered being told that it would bleed profusely if the cut was deep but she never imagined she would ever find herself having to deal with this amount of blood. All her training on that course slowly started coming back to her and she could even remember the exact words the trainer had spoken about when they were discussing severe injuries and bleeds in particular - to put direct pressure on the injury and to make sure that the person was in the correct treatment position because if they were not, they were more likely to die from the effects of shock because of the severe blood loss.

She remembered the First Aid trainer telling them on the course that when individuals with severe wounds had tried to continue running or walking to safety, instead of just laying still in the correct position, the considerable amount of blood loss that they were haemorrhaging out of their body had resulted in their demise because the heart no longer had a sufficient network of blood to pump around the body and so it simply stopped.

She remembered the trainer emphasising that if there was a wound inflicted to the head or chest area then the injured person should have to be positioned sitting up, "head or chest, up is best", those were the exact words the trainer had used she recalled. However "any wound below the diaphragm laying down is best" that was exactly what the First Aid trainer had impressed upon them. These words, somehow, had become imprinted in her memory and those were the exact instructions she had followed in order to help this stranger. He had been bleeding quite badly from the side, near his abdomen area and though she had not witnessed the event, she had come across him staggering towards her, clutching his side.

She had immediately acted to stem the flow of blood without any consideration for her safety.

It was funny. She marvelled at how the brain automatically delved deep into the memory banks to bring out the information that was relevant for this precise moment at exactly when it was needed, without any hesitation.

Oh God she prayed to herself "PLEASE let that ambulance come right now …I don`t think I can wait any longer".

She was not sure that she had heard the stranger correctly the first time round… she was aware that whenever anyone suspected that they were under any threat, their senses would become highly attuned and she wondered to herself if she had just imagined it…. what was it he had said …"don`t tell anyone, or your life will be in danger?" Was that what he had said or had she been hearing things….but now there was no misunderstanding the urgency of his pleas because his next words, though spoken softly, sent an even deeper chill down her spine.

"Listen to me, you`ve helped me enough, now GO, run while you can because if they catch up with you, you will be dead. They will coerce you into telling all sorts of lies about me and if you don`t listen to them your life will be ruined. Please, if you don`t want to listen to me then listen to your intuition, it will guide you to the truth, now go, but don`t tell anyone what I have just said." His eyes beseeched her and silently mouthed again, the words

"GO"......he tried to push her away but it was a faint shove and she thought she could feel his strength ebbing away from him. "I can hear the sirens now, I will be OK but you HAVE to go now" he begged, with even more urgency.

An eerie silence enveloped her and it felt as though she was all alone with this stranger who seemed to be slowly slipping away in front of her eyes and she suddenly felt a sense of helplessness as though there was nothing more she could do for him now.

Without warning, a deep sadness engulfed her, so sudden was it that it was like being pulled into a deep dark void that had no end. At that moment all she wanted to do was to lay down beside him and die with him. If everything came to an end right now, she would no longer have to worry about anything, she thought.

She felt a deep connectedness to him, for no apparent reason and she was determined not to leave him in what may be his final moments on this earth. At least he would have someone to have comforted him and he would not be alone.

She was hoping that his imminent death was just a figment of her hypersensitive imagination. From what she had seen, she was unsure if he would pull through this ordeal and just as she would not want to be left alone in a similar situation she was determined not to abandon him at this crucial moment without him knowing that someone was going to be there to comfort him.

She could not understand how a stranger could influence her so deeply having only just met him so briefly and under such tumultuous circumstances but that was precisely how she felt.

It was only later that she realised that she was such an empath that his emotions were affecting her now.

Chapter 2

Out of the corner of her eye a movement caught her eye
and as she looked up she saw two men fast approaching.
Her first thought was "Thank God some-one is coming".

However that thought was soon banished and turned to
something more sinister and fearful when she noticed
from where she was that they were coming towards her
with a sense of purpose and menace.

Her gaze moved away from their eyes falling down
towards the floor but not before she noticed a glint in the
palm of their hands, as the sun's reflection hit the
metallic object that they were both holding. For some
reason, she could not move her gaze at all, her eyes were
glued at their approach and the indistinguishable items in
their hand.

As they came closer there was no mistaking what it was
that they were both holding but also trying at the same
time to conceal unsuccessfully. She recognised the dark
black outline of a revolver in each of their hands and the
look on their faces as they approached could not hide the
anticipation of dread she had felt earlier on, as a shiver of
pure fear coursed through her whole being, a feeling
worse than death she thought.

It made the words the stranger had spoken earlier appear
to ring so true now and she immediately stood up and
turned to flee in the opposite direction but before she had
taken a single stride, they were upon her as one of them
caught hold of one of her outstretched hands stopping her
in her tracks and preventing her from running away.
Caught in his stranglehold she stood rooted to the

ground, unable to move one way or the other.

She was glad she had quickly pocketed the piece of paper the stranger had given to her before they had approached and she was sure that they had not arrived early enough at the scene to witness the event that had unfolded in what seemed like seconds ago.

As she tried, once again, to twist away from his clutches, a shout rang out from the gathering crowd which had suddenly appeared from nowhere. Their attention had now become focussed on the events in front of them where the injured man lay on the floor beside her and where she was being manhandled by the stranger.

The onlookers had misinterpreted the scene and must have thought that these two men were attacking both her and her friend who was on the floor. They started closing around the two men, forming a circle around them to protect her and the stranger, effectively creating a shield between them.

This was the distraction she needed because the man who had earlier taken hold of her so forcefully, suddenly loosened his grip on her, giving her the opportunity to rush into the crowd and push herself into the throng to become lost amongst them.

Out of the corner of her eye she saw the two men hiding their weapons and flashing some form of I.D. badges but she did not wait to find out who they were or what they were doing there.

She suspected that it was something to do with the injured stranger but for the moment her whole attention was on trying to escape from them, so instead of lingering around to observe the final outcome of her entanglement with the stranger, she continued moving as far away from the scene as possible, without drawing attention to herself.

As she pushed herself further into this mass of humans who had suddenly appeared, she realised that this was a demonstration that she had read about in the local paper earlier at breakfast. She also vaguely remembered the concierge at the hotel telling her to avoid this part of the street at this time of day due to skirmishes between the demonstrators and the police but she could not recollect what he had said or the reason for this mass of people coming together so suddenly.

Fortunately no violence had erupted yet as she made her way through the throng and the placards they were holding up gave her adequate cover to escape without being seen by the two men. She was relieved to notice as she moved amongst them that they were a light-hearted and jovial crowd, with no intention of causing trouble, far from what she had been told or read about, in the paper, earlier in the day, as she silently thanked them for inadvertently coming to her rescue.

She left the crowd and stepped away from the direction in which the throng was travelling and started to make her way back to the hotel.

Her heart was still beating rapidly and her thoughts were running so fast in her head that she had to tell herself to calm down and to breathe slower. As she was walking, people she passed were giving her some strange and even questionable looks, avoiding her as she approached them. Unsure why they were reacting in this way she looked down in order to avoid their gaze and as she did she so, she understood why.

Her freshly laundered pink cardigan which she had placed around her shoulders to keep her warm, when she had left her hotel after breakfast, was covered in the strangers` blood. She remembered that she had used part of it to stem his bleeding but she had not noticed how badly stained it was when she had put it back on. Her heart had still been pounding in her ears and she must have looked a spectacle with her tossed hair, dishevelled appearance and a somewhat vacant look. The blood-stained cardigan just attracted even more unwanted attention, to boot, so she quickly removed it and folded it into her arms, making sure no bloody part of it was visible and continued walking towards her hotel. Any onlookers would see it as a natural reaction to the heat of the day, as she already looked the part and she was hoping that it would help to make her feel less hot in this heat, which now felt a little oppressing for her.

She felt the sun`s rays on her whole body and that with her fast pace caused her to feel uncomfortable as her body started to heat up even more. Her bare arms and legs were beginning to swelter in the heat, as she felt a moistness beginning to form in her underarms and cleavage. It was making her feel a little faint now and the fact that she had not eaten well at breakfast only compounded the feeling as a little dizziness began to swirl around her head and the hot air started to suffocate her.

She walked across the road where shadows were now forming and where the sun`s rays were unable to penetrate these towering building blocks of stone and glass. The shaded area offered her some respite and she felt her body begin to cool down now. Thankfully the move provided her with some much needed comfort and, at the same time, it gave her an element of privacy in this semi-darkness as she continued back towards her hotel. By remaining in the shadows she thought that she would not be noticed as much and she even slowed down her pace pretending to look at the shop windows at various points. She glanced back furtively, making sure that she was not being followed and paying close attention to any reflections that may appear in the shop window of any suspected stalker but she did not notice anything to cause suspicion.

She continued walking in deep thought trying to put the pieces of her experiences together but none of it made any sense to her.

Why would the stranger tell her not to help him when it was clear to see that he was in need of assistance… and why were the police after him…was he a convicted felon who had escaped….but then why would the two men have disguised their weapons once the crowd came upon them …and were they really policemen or were they carrying false identifications like they do in the movies. All these thoughts kept churning inside her mind and she was getting herself into a chaotic mental tangle, letting her imagination get the better of her.

She realised that if she continued like this she would trigger her migraines which always developed when she placed undue stress upon herself and she certainly would be no closer to a satisfactory answer.

Besides she had come here to take a short break and

make the most of the wonderful weather at this time of the year. She was always drawn to nature and all its variety of vibrant displays, a complete contrast to her dull and insipid office environment which often felt suffocating.

The scenery could be breath-taking one moment and devastating another moment and it did not faze her as she loved being outdoors no matter the weather.

As yet she had not had the opportunity to enjoy any of the beautiful scenery outdoors that this part of the world was renowned for, so she decided to put a stop to the conflict that was brewing inside of her and make better use of the short time that was remaining.

Perhaps in the safety and comfort of her hotel room, after cleaning herself up and then gathering her thoughts she could make better sense of all this and not jump to any silly conclusions, she thought.

Chapter 3

The sense of fear had not left her and she was still afraid that she was being followed even though she could not see anyone each time she peered at the reflections in the shop window so she started walking faster, her feet automatically propelling her body forward.

She was glad she had worn these Sketchers as the shoes absorbed the shock of feet thumping the ground. The pounding that she was giving her feet as she increased her pace in an effort to move faster would not have been possible in any of the other shoes she owned and she was glad that she had decided to throw these into her suitcase at the last moment.

She was sure that anyone following would have to match her pace and she was in relatively good shape to maintain that speed all the way to the hotel if she needed to as she regularly exercised to keep fit, swimming or walking every day to ensure that her stamina levels were very good.

She was thankful that she had consulted a map before she had decided to go for a short stroll this morning from her hotel and she remembered the longer and diversionary route that would take her back to her hotel so that if anyone was following her they would not know where she was heading as the road led to a variety of hotels on the way. She could not recall how long she had been walking or what time of day it was now, as she paused for a moment to catch her breath and even though she had tried to calm herself, the words the stranger had spoken kept reverberating in her mind over and over again. Her senses had been in a really heightened state since that encounter and that alertness had still not left her. She had intentionally chosen this route because she felt she was walking in relative safety on this street which was lined with shops and strollers so she would not be alone at any point making it virtually impossible to attack her without any one witnessing the events.

Nonetheless, she felt that eyes were watching her every movement even though she had not seen anyone suspicious and no-one appeared to be behind her so she slowed down her pace and tried to get her breath back, breathing a bit more slowly and steadily. She hadn`t realised that the events had made her so tense and that her breathing had become short and sharp, matching the tenseness she was still feeling.

As she turned the corner she could just about make out the large sign at the top of the building of her hotel to tell her that she was nearing safety. She breathed out a huge gasp of air as she climbed the small steps to the hotel, more because she was glad to be back in one piece than anything else, and it was even more of a relief, when she approached the entrance door to the hotel and the doorman opened it, to allow her in.

She paused to allow him to open the door fully and casually glanced behind her to confirm that she had not been followed.

There was no-one lurking near the steps and as she walked into the hotel a cry of laughter or something close to it escaped from her lips. She realised that the doorman must have heard her because the expression on his face altered, from a welcoming smile, to one of curiosity or concern, she was not sure which, as she looked up at him but he said nothing. Instead he continued to hold open the door to let her through and a smile returned to his face.

Of all the things to make an impact on her, it was this small gesture that finally made her relax and feel a sense of calmness return, something she had not felt since her encounter with the stranger.

She was glad now that when she had been browsing the internet she had chosen to stay at this hotel because it still maintained some of the old-fashioned courtesies of keeping a doorman at the front of the entrance to allow guests in and out and, at the same time ensuring no uninvited guests were allowed in. Rather like a bouncer at plush parties or in clubs, you knew that you were in relative safety when there was a guard outside your door, preventing any unwelcome visitors.

The doorman was dressed in a long black coat with matching trousers. The coat had gold trimmings on the sleeve which matched the trimmings on the top hat that he also wore. His clean white shirt and red tie gave the impression that he was in total control and ready to spring into action if the need arose. As he raised his hat to her and bowed, she felt even more comforted and secure by this gesture, not knowing why though, as she made her way to reception to collect her keys.

The lobby area was expansive and fully air-conditioned and there was comfortable seating spread around in groups of two and three. Sofas were evenly positioned, accompanied by glass covered round tables that were perfectly placed so that if one wanted to read a book or newspaper, or even just have some coffee, one could do so without feeling cramped. The walls were tastefully painted with neutral pastel shades and here and there paintings of landscapes that reflected the local area hung on walls to make the whole space feel lavish but not ostentatious and this summed up the ambience of the hotel.

Without her cardigan, the air-conditioning inside the hotel lobby felt cold and the slight chill made the hairs in her arms rise up so she did not loiter too long, only sufficiently to notice if anyone had followed her into the hotel.

No-one else came through the doors so after collecting her smartcard key for her room from the receptionist, she made her way to the lifts and pressed the floor to which her room was located. She willed the doors to the lifts to close more quickly and for them to transport her even faster onto her floor, so that she could just go into her room and fall onto the bed and shut herself off from the World if only, for a moment. She stood patiently for the lift to take her to her floor and she was glad nobody else stopped its progress, as it climbed slowly upwards. She was thankful she was all alone in there at the moment, as she was in no mood for any small talk with strangers.

The whirring throng of the lift as they shifted into gear reminded her of the whirring of helicopter blades hovering in the sky and her trip to USA. She had gone hiking and camping with friends in her first year at University, to the Grand Canyon National Recreation Area around Horseshoe Bend, near the town of Page,

Arizona. Its vastness and stunning beauty, although no match for her current environment, made you forget about all the worlds` problems as the Canyon stretched out into, what felt like infinity. The depth of the gorges and the river below as it weaved its course beyond the horizon could not be a scenery one could easily forget. After seeing the view from close up they had saved enough money to take a helicopter ride to get a different perspective from a higher vantage point and they weren`t disappointed. The stunning photos they had taken as the helicopter hovered above this magnificent Natural Wonder of the World was evidence that they had taken the best decision to view it from both those angles. It always reminded her how Nature always inspired her and lifted her spirits, something that nobody else had succeeded in doing so far.

The lift finally stopped at her floor and as the doors slowly opened to allow her out, she was jolted back to the present. As she exited, she walked into the narrow dark hallway towards her room, a musty smell invading her nostrils. It bought back memories of her first year at the University Campus and the corridor that led to her room, which had a similar odour too. As she continued walking, she noticed that dotted around the hallway walls, hung smaller landscape pictures from local artists, each representing different areas of the coastline. She would have loved to have inspected them more closely but she was more intent in getting to her room and getting out of her clothes. In the distance she could hear a vacuum thrumming and realised that the hotel cleaner was doing her rounds. She hoped that the cleaner would not be interrupting her and just to be certain reminded herself to place the "Do Not Disturb" placard out on the door handle of her room.

As she approached her room number she swiped her key card at the entrance and heard it click as the door automatically opened to allow her access inside. For a moment she was blinded by the sun`s light as it shone so brightly through the large windows into her room and she had to pause a moment to allow her eyesight to adjust to it. She remembered drawing open the curtains, earlier in the morning before her walk, to allow the sun to naturally warm up the room and she was glad she had done that as it gave her a warm, safe feeling.

She headed straight for the bathroom and she began to discard her clothes onto the bathroom floor because she could smell the stranger`s blood on her, even though there were no signs of it on her skin. Her clothes felt dirty, with a hint of the smell of sweat as she had been almost running, to escape the men. The material had stuck to her like glue, when she had been walking so fast and now all she desperately wanted to do, was to get out of them and into a hot relaxing bath, to ease away all the tension that she had been holding onto since meeting the stranger and to try and forget everything that had just happened.

Chapter 4

She could not recall how she ended up on the bed but she must have fallen fast asleep without eating.

As she opened her eyes to welcome another new day she noticed that she was wearing the bath robe that she had changed into after her bath and it now hung loosely on her with the belt untied and drooping on either side of the straps.

Her eyes wondered around the room and she was surprised to find she had slept through to the next day. She realised that she must have been exhausted after her excursions but she could not recall why.

Then it suddenly dawned on her just as the sun`s rays were forcing her to fully open her eyes as the shaft of light piercing through the room where she was sleeping became so bright that she could no longer keep her eyes closed.

It was as though she was being forced to wake up and as she lay fully awake now in the bed she recalled the events of the previous day.

For a moment she wondered if she had dreamt it all.

As her gaze fell to the blood-stained cardigan lying on the floor beside her she realised with a sense of dread that this was not the case, it was not a nightmare, the events had truly transpired.

She needed time to recall the exact events of the previous day so she lay in bed for a few moments more, trying at the same time to work out a plan of action.

The stranger had clearly cautioned her not to speak to anyone and she could not understand why.

If only there had been more time to interrogate him further, she was certain that she would not have to be so worried and that he had exaggerated his concern for her.

She wondered whether he had survived his injuries. Perhaps if she could contact him now she could find out a bit more about him and how he had sustained those injuries in the first place. The envelope he had given her may be the clue so she jumped out of bed and dug furiously in her cardigan pockets to retrieve it. She felt the envelope in her hands and it weighed very light, too light to have anything inside it so she moved next to the window and held it up in the bright sunshine to see if she could discover its contents but she was deeply disappointed to see nothing around its frame.

As she bent the envelope very slightly, she rattled it to see if the contents would move around inside but her suspicions were confirmed. The stranger had given her an empty envelope with just an address on it.

How could that possibly be a threat to anyone she thought.

What could she do to discover the truth? She was unsure of what to do next.

Perhaps if she rang the hospitals nearby and claim that she was a relative of his, she could find out if he was alive.

This may raise suspicions if the police were guarding him and the staff may alert them to the call and if they were to trace it she would be discovered she thought. At least she would be relieved to know that he was fine and it might help her from jumping to any silly conclusions, she thought but then again, they might think that she was the attacker and that would only raise more questions than answers so she had second thoughts.

She did not want to do anything to compromise her own safety and could not think of a way to do anything without drawing attention to herself but she knew she had to do something but she just could not think at that moment.

Her stomach started rumbling, reminding her that she had eaten nothing since breakfast the day before. She knew she worked better on a full stomach. In the past she was always finding answers to any solution, big or small after a good meal. So she dressed and went down for breakfast.

She chose a table where there were only two seats and to ensure that no-one else would sit next to her she placed a cardigan and handbag next to where she sat making it clearly obvious to all that she wished to be left alone. The view she chose from where she was seated, allowed her to observe whoever was coming in and out of the hotel restaurant. She could observe them closely so that it would become apparent to her, if any-one was acting strangely and she would certainly recognise the two men who had approached her with such menace the previous day.

The majority of the individuals at this hotel were tourists dressed in holiday clothing and they were all relaxed and acting friendly, exchanging brief pleasantries before seating themselves at their tables for breakfast so she was sure she would notice anything amiss.

The few businessmen that were at the table seemed to be in a rush and quickly chose their breakfast from the bar and raced back to their table devouring it so fast before exiting that she was sure none of them could be counted as suspicious.

Having satisfied her hunger she decided to go for a short walk after breakfast to take in the sea air and allow her head to clear and give her ideas as to what to do next. She handed in her key at the front desk and walked towards the seafront.

She was glad now that she had chosen this hotel, once again as it was so close to the sea even though it was slightly more expensive than the others she had considered. She had felt it was a treat that she deserved after all the hard work she had done this year. The smell of the sea in her nostrils always felt refreshing and inspired her and as she inhaled deep breaths of air, she started to feel a little invigorated by the sea air.

She continued walking along the promenade, just enjoying this moment of peace.

There were few tourists at this time of day but she was not alone, strolling along the shore, so she felt safe. Nonetheless, she stayed within sight of them, just as a precaution.

Being here always bought back fond memories of her Childhood. She vaguely remembered living by the sea, roaming around near the waters` shore looking for the tiny things that dwelt in the rock-pools and exploring all the nooks and crannies nearby. It was a place she truly felt at home, probably because of the freedom of being in the open, fresh air, feeling the wind on your face and the smell of the salty water. The memory had obviously left a deep imprint on her mind and whenever she felt troubled she would return to the coast and always find the right answers to her problems and she was hoping that today would be no different.

It was a beautiful sunny day again and the smell of the salty sea breeze with the sound of the screeching of seagulls in the distance, lulled her into a sense of security as she continued walking.

She went down a slope and came onto the beach. Her feet crunched on the soft white sand as her shoes made contact and left indented imprints on it. She was tempted to take off her shoes and run with her hands outstretched to the sky as she had done when she was a little girl with no care in the world but she knew that she had to find a solution before returning to her hotel. She walked the stretch of the beach in total silence and cut out all sounds around her apart from the waves breaking on to the shore, splaying outwards as if gently caressing the ground on which they touched so briefly and then rapidly turning back to the sea. She paused and watched the movement of the waves coming up to the shore and then receding back down to reconnect with the large expanse of water again, like a baby taking its first steps out into the world and then retreating back into the safety of its mothers` arms. As she continued watching the ebb and flow of the tide she felt herself gently swaying side to side, matching the movement of the water and becoming hypnotised at the same time.

If only she could stand here like this forever she thought but she had to make a decision.

She turned back and retraced her steps.

The sun`s rays on her back warmed her body as she felt

a sense of comfort and well-being and she headed towards a bench where she sat down to relax and gather her thoughts. In this calm mood she decided to go to the police and report everything she had seen.

After all, the stranger could have been mistaken by what he had warned her about. She was aware that when anyone has life threatening injuries their senses are on high alert and so may say things that are a little far-fetched she thought to herself. Now that she had time to relax and process the events of the previous day things seemed far less grave and she no longer felt threatened. She had been very careful so far and no-one was watching her or following her so she was sure that she had come to the right decision.

She stood up to go back to her hotel room to collect her purse so that she could show them her identity if they needed it. In her rush to clear her head and go for her walk, she had forgotten to pick it up and the hotel was not that far away so she decided to return and ask the concierge for directions to the police station at the same time.

Chapter 5

It was still fairly early in the morning and the traffic was very light as she walked towards the edge of the pavement waiting for the cars to pass her before she crossed over.

A dark black car with darkened windows was approaching slowly, and she thought it looked unusual as most of the cars here were open topped or rentals. She had recognised this earlier when she had gone for a walk as the logos of the car hire companies on the sides of the windscreen were clearly evident. This was, after all, a popular tourist area but it was not quite the height of summer so one could move around without being hindered by tourists standing in the middle of the street trying to find their way around an unfamiliar place.

Once again she felt no sense of danger as there were a handful of people around with some tourists taking pictures and if she happened to be kidnapped at least there would be some physical evidence from those photographs, she thought, should there be the need. Besides she did not think any-one would try anything in broad daylight but she did notice that the car seemed to be taking a long time for it to move past her. However, before she could take another step forward two men rapidly came out of the front and back passenger side and man-handled her into the car. These were the very men, she had seen the previous day, and a sense of panic suddenly came rising to the surface and a scream started at her throat but it had become so dry suddenly that nothing but a gentle moan came out. She was pushed into

the passenger side of the car and as the car started off she
started to reach for the door handles on her side to escape
but her arm was quickly restrained by one of the men
sitting next to her.

She was sure that someone must have witnessed these
events and that a police car would be immediately
summoned and come screaming with sirens blaring to
chase them down at any moment but the silence in the car
only made her fear the worst as all manner of dark
thoughts started taking shape as she let her imagination
run wild once again. After all no-one knew where she
was or where she was going as she hadn`t felt the need to
tell anyone and she now wished she had taken better
precautions, especially as the stranger had warned her
that her safety may be at risk if she did not leave him.

However her fears were allayed slightly when one of the
men held out an identification badge in front of her and
told her that they were detectives from some special unit
and that she had been taken for her own safety. They
proceeded to tell her that her life was in danger because
she had come into contact with the stranger and they
were going to take her to the local police station as a
temporary measure until a better solution could be
arranged.

She had not been handcuffed or restrained in any way
and was informed that, if afterwards, she wanted to leave
she could do. However, they wanted to share some
important information with her about the stranger so she
could draw her own conclusions about him.

They still appeared menacing and she could not get the
feeling of insecurity out of her system despite their

assurances so for the moment there was no choice but to follow and surrender to their demands.

For the time being anyway, she surrendered and let herself be driven to the station. However she made a mental note of where they were taking her just in case she needed to escape but the fact that they had not blindfolded her or tied her up bought her some sense of temporary comfort.

They approached a rather ancient and forbidding building with large pillars on either side with steps leading to a large locked door. The only clue as to its identity was an illuminated blue sign above it with the words "police station". Below and to their right was an arched entrance where police cars and larger vans were parked so she had no doubt that the officers were telling the truth. As they walked into the building there was a long narrow hallway straight ahead and to the side was an open desk, rather like a receptionist desk. There was a sergeant at the desk, she could tell this because he had three stripes on the side of his uniform and as she passed him he merely looked up for a brief second and without acknowledging her looked down again making himself look busy with some papers he had on his desk.

She was taken into the station but there were no other uniformed officers around and the thought crossed her mind that perhaps they were out on duty, still dealing with the aftermath of the demonstrations of the previous day making sure their presence was felt so that there would be no further trouble. She may have been mistaken but a look of worry or something else had passed across the sergeant`s face as she was led to the end of the hallway and into a windowless room and as she was escorted in she felt as though she was a prisoner being interrogated for a serious crime. The feeling continued when she was asked to sit at a table facing the two men who had escorted her from the car and into the building in order to answer some questions. She was certainly no criminal and being treated like one immediately put up her defences so that when they started asking her questions she point blankly refused to answer anything until they told her why she was being held here.

Hearing her unhelpful responses they changed tack and started to be less provocative by firstly explaining why she had been bought here. They explained that the person she had assisted was in fact an escaped prisoner who had stolen some valuable information that posed a threat to the stability of the security in this country and she could not be told too much because of confidentiality. Their earlier excuse in detaining her was merely a ruse to try to calm her down and make sure she would come willingly into the car they added, she was not really in any danger but they had to make sure that she came. She hurled all manner of questions at them but every question she had for them remained unanswered and the excuse was always the same, because of the threat to national security.

She was pleased, however, when they informed her that the stranger she had saved had recovered from his injuries in hospital and whilst being treated there had managed to escape.

She was beginning to feel a little weary with their line of questioning which was bordering on bullying and she wanted a break from all their accusations.

They were intimating to her that she would be imprisoned as an accomplice if she continued being unhelpful but she was unable to answer any of their questions.

If anything she was mentally gleaning from their line of questioning some information about the stranger and his circumstances and she mentally stored it away for the future should she meet him again.

They realised they were not getting very far and so one of them went out whilst the other one remained in the room in silence just staring at her. His partner returned shortly with cups of tea and biscuits and their attitude slowly shifted and she felt the ice starting to melt after the refreshments.

When the questioning started again the tone shifted and they became sympathetic towards her so she began to explain what had happened from beginning to end but omitting the detail about being handed the piece of paper and the warning from the stranger. They in turn wanted to establish exactly what had taken place between the two of them in detail and kept asking her the same questions in a different format to ensure she was telling the truth.

She had already been asked to disclose some basic information about her that they could verify such as her name, address, occupation and she realised she had given the information freely without thinking of the possible repercussions and wondered if she needed to have a lawyer present but that would only exacerbate the situation and they may consider that she had something to hide if she did ask for one. Her personal information could easily be elicited from other sources and it was too late now to hold back, in any case, what harm could it possibly do she thought, as they were policemen, or some form of law enforcement officers (that she had never heard of) after all.

After what felt like a long time the tone of the conversation then changed and she felt a chill in the air as some more queries started, always though, about the same thing. They asked her if she was being truthful with them and what her relationship was to the victim and how they had met and it now crossed her mind how quickly it had taken them to identify her as his rescuer.

The cautionary words the stranger had spoken now came back to her but she continued answering the questions in as truthful a note as possible hoping they would not hear anything amiss. She repeated that she was just an innocent by-stander who had come across the stranger and had merely come to his rescue, she just happened to be in the wrong place and time, or from the stranger's perspective in the right place at the right time. She was here on holiday for a few days and would be returning home and this could be clearly proven by the hotel where she was staying.

She obliged them with all their questions and they finally seemed to be accepting that her words rang true.

The conversation then turned to words the stranger may have spoken to her but she innocently replied that she had been so shocked by the amount of blood and the severity of his injuries that she could not recall anything he had said. Eventually when they exhausted all their lines of questioning she asked to go back to her hotel as she really could not elaborate any further.

She was allowed to leave and as she had no purse or money on her was escorted back to the hotel in the same car. Before departing they warned her not to discuss the meeting with anyone and gave her a telephone number on a crumpled piece of paper in order to contact them, in case she was able to recall any further information. The way she had been manhandled into the car and her subsequent initial interrogation, being treated like a criminal gave her little enthusiasm to even want to have anything to do with them but as she stepped out of the car one of the men sitting beside her took hold of her hand and drew her close to him as he quietly whispered a veiled threat that gave her no doubt as to the repercussions if she did not obey their command and once again she felt a shiver of fright running down her spine as she rushed to get out of their clutches and into the safety of her hotel room where she could ponder the day`s events.

She had no intention of ever contacting them again and wanted to erase this experience from her memory and her initial reaction was to throw the piece of paper into the gutter where it belonged but for her own safety she decided to keep it until the time proved right to dispose of it.

Chapter 6

When she arrived at the reception desk to pick up her keys she was interrupted by one of the tour guides who assumed she was ready to be collected to board the coach for a tour of the area.

With all that had passed in the last few days she had completely forgotten about having arranged the sight-seeing tour when she had arrived at the hotel but now she felt she could not cancel it as it was too late to do so. Although she was not in the mood for it she felt that if anyone was watching her she wanted them to think that she had nothing to hide and everything was as much back to normality as possible so she picked up some things from her room and accompanied the tour guide onto the bus.

She sat next to an elderly woman who was very chatty and this distracted her from her present predicament. The tour took in some architectural places of interest and the guide was explaining some of the history behind the places they were visiting but nothing stayed in her head, everything passed as though she was in a haze. They had stopped for souvenirs and lunch and continued the tour until the early part of the evening and if anyone were to ask her about the tour she could not recollect anything the guide had said.

Usually she had a great deal of interest in the places she visited and was always awed by the architecture and especially the antiquities of the region but today she was just grateful for the distraction the tour had afforded her as the bus made its way back to the hotel.

As she collected her hotel key again she realised that she was really tired and was glad that she had two more days left of her holiday before driving back home as it was a long journey and she needed some rest.

She collected her room key and took the lift to the fourth floor, instead of climbing the stairs, as she normally did. She swiped the card at her door and as she opened it and placed the key into the slot to power up the room and bring some light into it she could not believe the scene she was seeing and it took a few seconds to register the utter chaos in front of her.

Chapter 7

She was shocked to see all her belongings thrown out of their drawers and onto the floor, nothing had been left untouched. All her clothes (there were not that many) were scattered in all directions with the two empty suitcases flung in separate corners of the room and to make matters worse her hand and face creams were emptied onto the clothes so that they were stained and ruined, unwearable now.

Her shoes and slippers had been slashed through with a knife and even her underwear, nightwear, stockings and make-up had not been left unscathed, in fact, everything they could get their hands on had been trashed and the whole room was in an utter mess.

She just felt devoid of all emotion with everything that had happened over the last few days and she now sorely wished she had not come here at all but instead spent some time at home relaxing.

The scene in front of her was too overwhelming and the violence of what was in front of her brought her to her knees as tears welled up and flowed uncontrollably down her face as her body shook in utter helplessness. It was as though she had been punched in the stomach and all the energy drained out of her body, there was nothing but emptiness left inside. She felt that her personal space had been invaded and she had been physically violated, and an anger that she had never felt, begun to erupt deep inside.

After what seemed like several minutes she decided that whoever was responsible for this was not going to get the better of her and she would not surrender to their attempt at undermining her, after all she was made of sterner stuff and she would show them that she remained unaffected by their intimidation.

It took all of her effort to wipe the tears from her eyes and walk cautiously to the bedside table to try to avoid disturbing anything and she picked up the phone in order to ring the receptionist and ask her to call the hotel security and the police.

The words coming out of her mouth sounded like someone else`s, it was as though a machine was talking without her registering anything of what was spoken, the words just flowed automatically out and once she finished the call, she sat by the bed with her door ajar, to allow the security personnel in.

She did not have the energy to call to them when they entered as she was so dazed and feelings of rage continued to well up deep inside her, almost like a volcano ready to erupt at any moment. How dare anyone come into this room and invade and destroy it like this, she thought. She felt such anger and could easily kill the person who had done this if he or she were standing in front of her right now.

Hotel security could do nothing about the mess or break-in and decided to call the Hotel Manager in an attempt to placate her and offer a solution. Before he arrived though, two men in Police uniforms identified themselves and whilst one of them started looking for clues as to who may have been responsible, the other one took out his notebook and proceeded to ask her questions. As she looked up to acknowledge their presence she recognised the desk sergeant standing in front of her. She had not moved from her position since discovering the ransacking and could not find the strength to get up to see what was missing and as he continued with his line of enquiries his tone of voice was so matter-of-fact that she had to remind him of her earlier visit to the police station. She was sure he would remember her as the visit was so recent but he did not acknowledge seeing her or the two detectives who had accompanied her. As he continued making notes she described the two detectives who had been with her but he still refused to accept that she had been at the station at all and to make matters worse he claimed there were no detectives based at the station under the description she had given. She was getting even more annoyed now so she dug out the crumpled piece of paper they had given her but this just added insult to injury as he continued to deny their existence. The crumpled piece of paper was no evidence of her visit as the usual procedure, he continued, for anyone coming to the station was to fill out an incident form, for which she would have been given a copy.

She continued to describe the building and the room in which she had been taken to for questioning and saw a flicker of recognition in the sergeant's eyes but this was quickly extinguished and no matter how much she insisted on the truthfulness of those events the more he denied everything.

She realised that she had unwittingly embroiled herself in some sort of plot because although he was able to confirm her description of the building, he continued to deny that she had been to the station or even been interviewed by any-one and she realised that she was not going to establish the truth and would visit the station later on the next day and ask for the detectives in person.

She was in no position to argue with him anymore and just futilely accepted his comments but she was reminded again of the words the stranger had spoken to her.

She was too exhausted by all the events since her stay at the hotel so she let them continue their processing of the room in order to carry out their own investigations but answered all their questions in monotones.

When they finished they suggested that she stay in another room but she wanted to salvage some of her clothes and as they left she picked herself up to try and tidy it up the best she could as they had advised her that there was nothing more that could be done. As she went through each item, she realised that nothing was salvageable and so she went into the bathroom to bring out the bin in order to get rid of the tatters of clothing.

She noticed that her blood-stained cardigan which she had washed and left hanging in the bathroom had been the only thing left untouched along with her toothbrush, bath shower gels, shampoos and towels that the hotel had provided and she was thankful for some small comforts.

This suddenly reminded her of the envelope the stranger had given to her and she was relieved to still find it hidden in the tiny crevice behind the work desk where she had managed to stuff into, before she had left in the morning and she could feel it safely tucked inside along with the strewn tissues. Anyone looking there would have mistaken it for rubbish and she was thankful that she had decided to keep it hidden and that the intruders had not found it because it only went to prove to her the truthfulness of the events that had transpired earlier. She retrieved it and read the address on it and wondered if this was what they were after because nothing else was missing from her room and she sighed a sigh of relief to herself both because it was safe and because she had not mentioned anything to the police about this.

The Hotel Manager had arrived just as the police had left and he was very conciliatory, offering her the room next door.

He noticed that all her clothes had been ruined and even offered to pay for a new wardrobe provided that she mentioned none of this incident to her fellow guests or give the hotel a bad press.

She was far too concerned with her predicament to worry about the repercussions that the hotel may suffer and she placated the manager and told him that he had nothing to worry about. After all she had stayed here on two previous occasions and had had a wonderful time and could not let this situation influence her opinion.

He was pleased to hear of this and told her that if she needed anything she could contact the desk reception and he would notify them that they would comply, within reason, with her requests.

She was becoming really tired after the days' events and she began to yawn. The Hotel Manager took this as a sign for him to leave and after asking his staff to arrange another room for her to stay in, he duly took his leave.

She decided then and there to deliver the piece of paper to the address on it and hope that that would finally be the end of this experience but not before she enjoyed the remainder of her stay.

Chapter 8

The next two days flew by as Bethany spent her time relaxing, swimming and spoiling herself with saunas massages and Jacuzzis followed by meals at different restaurants and cafes and just letting the world pass her by.

She now felt that she was being watched but as she could not see by whom continued to enjoy the present time she had because she would soon be returning to work and some degree of normality. The end of the short break finally arrived and she decided to take a detour before going home to post the envelope the stranger had given her. It would bring the whole episode to a close and she could then go back to her routine in the hope that whoever was watching her would come to realise that she had been an innocent party in the wrong place at the wrong time.

She had looked at the directions on Google Maps and found that the address she had to deliver the envelope to, was en-route to where she was returning so it was not going out of her way that much.

She started off at a reasonable time after checking out of her hotel. The staff had been really kind to her after the break-in and the manager had given her a discount for the remaining two days she had left of her stay. They felt responsible for the incident and so had even contacted the local clothes` chains for her to purchase new clothes at their expense and though she was very grateful for their assistance she could not really blame them for all the events. She was disappointed, however that the hotel did not have security cameras but she could not really blame them as this was a holiday resort which had tourists visiting all year round and the website had also indicated that this area was the safest when she had chosen her destination, so she left with a promise to return the following year.

She had decided to take her time driving along the motorway and ensuring that she would stop every couple of hours for a short break but it seemed to take her no time at all to arrive at the town where she was to deliver the envelope.

When she arrived at the address she was astonished to find a row of broken down old houses shorn of their windows and walls, exposed to the elements and the blackened decay that had set in was evidence that some time ago these houses had caught fire so that all that remained in some places was a pile of rubble.

There was no way to approach the houses as they had been cordoned off by a large wire boundary and a clear warning sign to ward off anyone from entering with a picture of an Alsatian dog and a separate notice stating that the premises were protected by round the clock security, although at the moment she could see no-one.

She took out the envelope to check the address again and when she input the information on her phone for directions she was guided to the spot where she was.

For a moment she was stunned into inaction, after all, she had followed the advice of the stranger and had told no-one about being handed the envelope and she had gone to great lengths to conceal it so that it could not be found.

Yet here she was at the address but unable to deliver it.

She sat in her car for a few moments to gather her thoughts and as she glanced into her rear view mirror she could see a security guard in the distance with an Alsation dog, walking beside him, held tightly by a very short leash. They were striding purposefully in her direction and so she immediately started her car and steadily followed the flow of the road. At a convenient point, where there was little traffic, she performed a U-Turn, and consulted her phone again pretending to look around as though she was lost.

It seemed to have worked because the Security Guard seemed to have lost interest in her and walked away from the direction in which he was approaching.

She finally made her way back home and she was glad as she turned the key in her door to be home safe and sound with no other distractions.

Chapter 9

In no time at all Bethany settled back into her routine at work and the demands of it. After a few weeks her short break and the incident with the stranger had been almost forgotten, although she still felt that she was being observed.

In a way she was relieved that her life had resumed the normality of before but there was a small part of her that craved to contact the stranger and get some more facts from him about what he had meant when he had stated that her life would be in danger. However, in order to avoid any complications in her life, she chose not to pursue any enquiries that may jeopardise her safety even though physically, she felt under no threat.

A sequence of events, however, shattered that illusion when, for no apparent reason, one day she was called in to her Director's office.

As far as she was concerned she was making a valuable contribution in her work as her mentor had commented on how well she was currently progressing and that she would be next in line for a promotion so she assumed that perhaps this was the reason she was called in to see him.

As she entered her Director's office his manner was unusually serious and she suspected the worst when he did not ask her to sit down but kept her standing.

As she stood in front of his desk waiting for him to tell her why she had been summoned here she felt like a little kid being called in to the Headmaster's office at school, about to be told off for some minor misdemeanour but what came next stunned her completely.

He informed her matter-of-factly that her services were no longer required and she was to vacate her position immediately as there had been a restructure in the firm and that the role she currently occupied was no longer needed. To soften the blow she would be leaving with three month`s severance pay with immediate effect.

She walked back to her desk in a state of complete shock unable to comprehend what was happening. She began to empty her desk of her personal belongings which she placed in a spare carrier bag that she always carried in case of emergencies, never entertaining the thought that this is what it would be used for.

As she turned around to speak to one of her closest colleagues who sat behind her to explain why she was leaving and to say her goodbyes she was interrupted by a security guard who had suddenly appeared as if out of nowhere. It was obvious that he had been called to escort her out of the building and her face began to turn red as she started breaking into a sweat, feeling a sense of guilt for no reason but also anger at this treatment. Her rage was boiling inside her and she felt as though she was about to explode. Instead of being treated with sympathy for losing her job, she was being treated like a criminal.

She had only ever witnessed scenes like this on T.V., where an employee had defrauded the Organisation, for whom they were working for. She felt as though she had been labelled a criminal without even being given an opportunity to tell her side of the story and shown the door rather unceremoniously. She felt so ashamed, though she had no reason to, that she wished the floor below her feet would just open and swallow her up. She had no doubt that other staff witnessing this scene must be assuming the worst of her, just as she would do, if she was in their position.

As she walked past the bemused faces, some familiar and others not so, she realised that she would never be able to hold her head up high if, by any small chance, she returned here.

However the finality of this, when the door was slammed in her face at the exit by the security guard who had accompanied her, could not make it any more clearer to her that she would never be welcomed back here. The security guard, who was just carrying out his orders, had no idea about her circumstances but was also making the wrong assumptions about her as he looked at her with disdain and turned his back on her as soon as he "dumped" her outside.

Her humiliation was compounded even further when she took a final look up at the familiar building where she had worked for the last ten years and saw inquisitive faces looking out of the window witnessing her dismissal.

She immediately turned around and with her carrier bag in one hand and her handbag in the other, she slowly trudged towards the underground station to make her way home.

She walked in a state of shock, not registering anyone or anything she passed. Like an automaton she arrived at the station and registered her ticket at the turnstile as it clicked to allow her in. She made her way to the platform and as the train approached inside the tunnel the wind that it generated in her face cooled her down a little but she was still feeling the shock and embarrassment of being escorted out of her workplace by a security guard. She could not understand why she had been targeted in this manner and she considered taking legal action against her firm but at the moment all she wanted to do was to go home. It seemed odd that once again she was in a position where she felt that only her home could offer her some sort of security and stability but she put the thought aside as she boarded the train. Some-one brushed past her but she paid no attention and took a seat as close to the doors as possible so that when her stop came she could quickly alight the train and walk the short distance home, as fast as possible.

As her stop approached she stood up and neared the exit doors of the train. Once again she had the feeling that she was being watched and she casually looked round but there were no faces that she had seen before and so she passed it off as a figment of her heightened imagination. She walked up the escalators and as she approached the turnstile to display her pass she opened her purse and suddenly realised that her credit card holder was missing. She was certain that she had it in her possession when she had left her workplace as she had checked the contents of her bag before leaving and it suddenly dawned on her that it must have been stolen when she was boarding the train and a stranger had brushed against her.

She had been so deep in her own thoughts that she had not noticed what had happened.

As soon as she exited the station she used her mobile phone to inform her credit card company of the incident and then reported the theft to the police.

She had kept her phone in her inside jacket pocket and was thankful that it was still safe.

It was only her credit card, along with two other store cards, that had been stolen. The store cards were unimportant as they accumulated bonus points and held no significant value, other than discounted offers.

Fortunately her credit card had not been used and so no money had been withdrawn from her account.

She was relieved when she reached her front door with no further distractions and she quickly walked in, closing the door shut behind her wanting to block out the tumultuous events of the day.

For the next few days she walked around the house like an automaton, not noticing what she was doing but eating, sleeping and carrying out her normal activities (except work) as though she was on holiday.

She could not think about her future, her mind could only cope with today, the present.

Looking at the future felt like staring at a blank wall, it just looked too bleak, dark and painful. The implications of losing her job at this moment felt too raw to contemplate as it was as though she was re-opening a gaping wound that had still not healed.

So for the next few weeks she was content to remain indoors in her own company, staring aimlessly at four walls with no conversation, just silence to keep her company.

She had intentionally decided to cut herself off from the outside world to avoid facing her current predicament and she had chosen to just bury her head in the sand to try to forget the emotional pain she was experiencing.

As the weeks passed the inertia was making her feel stifled and depressed and she realised that she missed the company of her work colleagues and the camaraderie they had built over the years. Work had given her a reason to live and a purpose in her life but now that had been cruelly taken away from her she felt helpless.

It was as though she was experiencing a bereavement, only the loss was not of any one but of something and she could not understand how it was possible to feel so bereft.

Old emotions that had long been buried were coming to the surface and she did not know how to deal with them. In the past she always faced challenging situations head on and always kept herself busy, being a hive of activity but this sedentary stage of her life was raising too many doubts in her mind and she was beginning to lose her self-confidence. This was a new side of her character that she neither recognised, nor knew how to deal with and there was no-one to ask for guidance.

The more she thought about it, the more she realised that if she continued like this, she would eventually become just like the very people she had criticised on daytime television shows. They seemed to have nothing better to do then create unhealthy relationships and habits and if she didn't watch herself carefully she would become a couch potato too throwing away all the discipline she had fought so hard to maintain.

This apathy had gone on for far too long enough and she decided it was time to take some firm decisions. She felt she had been singled out unfairly by her employers by being dismissed in this manner and decided to see an Employment Lawyer to discover if there was a case of unfair dismissal for them to answer for.

She gathered all the paperwork she had accumulated, whilst working, including diaries she had kept about interviews and other conversations relating to her progress, that she had discussed with her superiors. She was glad she had made notes and even though they may not be official documents, they were fair comments made about the state of the company and her position in it, giving the impression that her job was secure and that she was progressing very well. She felt that she had been given no indication that the company were restructuring their work-force and if anything there had been subtle hints to indicate that the company were going to be expanding and taking on more staff.

She had not contacted any of her colleagues and they had made no attempt to contact her, probably because of the impression they had gained when she had been escorted out of the building so suddenly and unexpectedly. She could not blame them for that reaction but a small part of her quietly wished that someone would have at least made an attempt to speak to her, to find out how she was coping and also to get her side of the story in establishing the truth. However, perhaps if they did, they would jeopardise their own jobs so she understood why they had not made any attempts to get in touch with her.

She put all these thoughts out of her mind and contacted an Employment Lawyer and made an appointment to go and see him the following week.

This decision was not one she had taken lightly because she was aware of the length of time these matters took to resolve as well as the exorbitant costs of a legal battle.

She was pitting her wits against a large conglomerate who would have a limitless source of money to throw at defending their reputation so it was a battle in comparison with David and Goliath but she was confident that she had the upper hand because she had kept meticulous records.

She gathered all the relevant paperwork to substantiate her claim, together with important documents which she normally kept in a safe and secure place at home.

She could not shake the feeling of some impending misfortune heading her way, especially after experiencing all the unsettling events since she had met the stranger, so with that in mind, she took copies of everything she needed and decided to store the original documents in a safe storage facility, where she was certain that security was tight. Apart from her driving license, she decided to keep vital documents such as her passport, share certificates, title-deeds for her house and other important paperwork together, so that they were easily accessible if the need ever arose.

Satisfied that she had made the correct decision, she kept herself busy with tasks that she had never completed because she had been too busy at work, making it her priority for the last nine years. So she cleared all the clutter in the house that she had accumulated over the years. The finishing result was four bags of black bin liner bags full of several pairs of shoes she had bought but never worn, some the same style but in different colours. Three pairs of trainers that were each purchased on a whim, to encourage her to keep fit by jogging or visiting the gym but which she never committed to regularly and so they lay at the back of her wardrobe.

Then there were the countless dresses, skirts and matching tops, some of which were so out of fashion now that she would have been ashamed to wear them. It was a shame that she had never worn them and she admitted to herself, that she had completely forgotten that they still hung in her wardrobe, worse still, displaying their price tags. Other sundry items like T-shirts and nick knacks that she had bought as souvenirs while on holiday completed the list.

She recalled that while she was working, she prided herself on her appearance and although not a real follower of fashion would shop at mid-range stores to appear well-dressed at work. Even when the firm moved to voluntary casual dress, she would always be formally dressed as would some of her other colleagues. They had gotten into the habit of dressing smartly and they had felt that if they came in wearing casual clothing, their attitude towards their work may change. If they were casually dressed perhaps they may become too relaxed and laid back and that would impact on their work too and they would not perform as efficiently.

They had briefly discussed it amongst themselves and decided that they preferred formal attire, as it imparted an air of Professionalism that casual attire would not and they felt that taking the extra effort to turn out well-dressed, gave them a psychological edge.

In any case, they had become used to dressing smartly

in the office and it was a pattern they preferred to uphold.

One of her colleagues, in particular, always seemed to have new suits or dresses and Bethany was sure that she had never seen her wear the same dress twice. Bethany concluded that her colleague was addicted to clothes shopping as she would often recount all the occasions that she had attended the various fashion shows, either in London or Paris. She had often wondered how her colleague could afford to even attend those events but she never asked her, as she felt it was none of her business but she herself, would never go to those extreme lengths in order to follow current fashion trends. Bethany was content with the High Street chains.

Her colleague had, once, confidently shared with her that it was the only way for her to ensure that she kept herself in touch with the newest fashion trends and Bethany suspected that she had even bought some items from those shows, although she had never confided to anyone about that. Her colleague always seemed to be one step ahead of everyone else when it came to clothes and Bethany often wondered how she was able to spend so much, as she was certain that the pieces were one of a kind. Bethany had decided if people wanted to spend money on clothes that would be worn once and then discarded, then that was their prerogative. She had never felt the need to go to those lengths and considered herself to be a moderate spender when it came to fashion but the fully loaded black bin liners now made her realise that perhaps in the past, she had spent more on clothes than she had thought. At least she had purchased items that she could afford to pay for and repay any credit that was due within the month, so that she would not be charged the exorbitant interest rates that some of the companies levied. All in all she was careful with her spending and rarely threw money away on a whim, except for the odd occasion, when she was on holiday and wanted to spoil herself.

She placed the black bags in the rear of the boot of her car, with the intention of donating them to charity in the next few days.

Satisfied that she had done all she could indoors she cleared all the weeds in her small garden, mowed the lawn and planted some colourful flowers and plants around the borders so that when she eventually finished, the whole place looked almost unrecognisable.

Keeping busy had always been a tonic for her in the past and the last few days proved to be no exception as she felt her spirits raised.

Next, she concentrated on smartening up her appearance in readiness for her appointment with the Employment Lawyer, by visiting a hairdresser as she had let her hair go since being sacked. Whilst she was at home she was too lazy to do anything with it and after brushing it every morning tied it in a bun. Now as she unknotted the bun, her hair fell beyond her shoulders and she could see that it had become overgrown, worse still, with a lot of split ends clearly visible and it made her appearance even more unruly. She wanted to display a professional approach when meeting the Employment Lawyer and not the wounded, vindictive employee, who was out for revenge because of the manner of her dismissal. Some may take that negative approach because of the manner of their treatment but it was not the trap she wanted to fall into, as it would be of no benefit to her in the long run.

She knew that first impressions were vital in these situations and she wanted to show that she was genuine and had a valid reason, to take this course of action.

Her scheduled appointment with the lawyers, in the next few days, gave her something specific to focus on and she was confident that with all the evidence she had accumulated, there would be a ruling in her favour when the matter was presented to a tribunal. She no longer wanted her old job back but she did not want anyone else to be treated the same way as her.

She felt that large Corporations should be held to account and have someone to answer to and she did not want them to get away with what she felt was unethical, bordering on unlawful.

Now she was glad that she had kept accurate records of all of her Annual appraisals, along with the notes she had made discussing various action plans.

On the appointed day, she took great care in dressing smartly, even going so far as making sure her shoes were polished. It reminded her of her first job interview when she had felt really nervous but realised afterwards that her anxiety had not been necessary because she had flown through the interview process without any major hiccups. After being offered and accepting that job she had settled easily into her role and moved to other companies and spent a happy number of years there, with no regrets, bar the recent set of events. She knew she had nothing to fear but she could not avoid the knots in the pit of her stomach and started taking long deep breaths to calm her nerves, which she continued to do, until the moment when she stepped into their offices.

She arrived there with plenty of time to spare as she always hated being late and made an extra effort to arrive at least fifteen minutes before she was due. If she was ever too early, she would walk around the surrounding area and she found that it had the result of calming her jittery nerves.

Her meeting appeared to be promising and she was assured that she stood a very good chance of a successful and favourable conclusion. The Lawyer would contact her again, within a few weeks, to give her a better idea of a plan of action and with that in mind, as she left their offices, she felt relieved and justified that she had made the correct decision to take the matter to court.

Finally, she felt that she was making some forward progress and now all she had to do was to wait for them to contact her.

She still continued her pursuit of finding employment but she was not going to hurry the process.

She was also contemplating pursuing a totally different career from her previous one in the Financial Industry and she knew that it would take her time to weigh up all her options.

Chapter 10

Weeks flew by and she was beginning to get a little concerned that she had not heard from the Employment Lawyer regarding her case.

Just as she was on the verge of contacting them she received a worrying message from the gentleman who had been assigned to her case.

She had been pottering around in the garden when her mobile phone rang. She went into the house to be able to hear the conversation clearly as the gentleman seemed to be speaking in whispers. She realised that he must have been ringing from a payphone and was surprised that it was not from his office but as his words rolled out she realised to her horror that her nightmare was continuing.

He told her, in whispered tones, that he suspected her files had been confiscated, after two men had one day turned up unexpectedly at his firm, claiming to be from the Internal Revenue and forced him to hand all the papers to them. He had had dealings with the revenue services on several occasions on behalf of his clients before and so suspected that they were not who they claimed to be. He had demanded that they furnish him with the proper documentation, so that he could submit to their request, as was the usual procedure and that he had no intention of disregarding client confidentiality rules as it would place him and his firm in jeopardy of legal suits and probable disbarment from the profession.

He was not willing to surrender to them, and realising this, they walked out of his office and into the offices of one of the partners of the firm. Within a few minutes, they had returned to his office, accompanied by one of the senior partners who had demanded that he comply with their request. After they had left, he had documented the incident and recorded a complaint against the senior partner so that he would not be blamed for the irregularity that had just transpired. A few days later, he had been summoned into the offices of another senior partner and informed that he was being given the opportunity to take early retirement with a generous leaving package that would keep him and his wife comfortable for the rest of their lives. He felt that he had been given no other option but to accept it, as he was informed in a brusque and brutal manner that his refusal would be interpreted as non-compliance and lead to immediate termination of his employment, followed by a legal lawsuit. This kind of bullying was alien to him and he would not have expected that of the firm with whom he had dedicated his whole working life to. He realised that that loyalty was meaningless now and that his many years of service with this firm had been blown away by that incident, an incident in which he had done nothing wrong.

He suspected that there was more to it than met the eye and a great injustice was about to occur but he did not want to stand aside and let it prey on his conscience without at least warning her of those series of events. He wanted to help her but did not feel he was properly equipped to deal with it and had for several days afterward mulled over it. He had come to the conclusion that at the very least she should be alerted to this conspiracy.

With that, he disconnected the connection but not before telling her to refrain from contacting him, or involving him any further with whatever it was that she was involved in.

He was apologetic but he had to protect himself and his wife, as they had also threatened him, if he continued to pursue assisting her in any way.

Bethany realised that there was a concerted attempt by persons unknown to ruin her life and she had no doubt now that it was because she had interceded on the stranger's behalf so many weeks ago.

Her decisive plan of action lay in tatters and she was no closer to getting to the bottom of why she had been dismissed from the company she had worked loyally for so many years.

It made her realise that everyone was indispensable no matter how hard they worked and that individuals could lose their whole livelihoods at the drop of a hat, at the discretion of their employer's whim. She was fortunate that she had a financial safety net that she could draw upon but many others lived on a day to day basis, hand to mouth, with no such security.

It made her appreciate the decisions she had made in the past to be in this relatively secure position and she had to at least be thankful that she was not out on the streets. She had a roof over her head and food on the table and that now felt more precious to her than at any other time in her life. The more she reflected upon it the more she was thankful that she was healthy, mobile and with an intact mental acuity. She had never wanted to be a burden to anyone, least of all, the state and as long as she had the financial means to support herself she felt she was on a good footing from which to spring from.

As she contemplated all this her thoughts were interrupted by a ringing. It was her mobile phone and to her surprise it was the Employment Lawyer`s calling her.

They asked her to come in that afternoon so that they could discuss her case. Without hesitation she immediately accepted the invitation and wondered if, perhaps, her fortunes had turned. She did not want to make any assumptions, however, as the conversation with their previous employee had put her on her guard and she decided to take a cautious approach and not give anything away until she was sure of their true intentions.

As usual she arrived there early and was lead into the reception area where she was invited to take a seat. A few minutes later another woman guided her into another office which was scantily furnished and was asked to take a seat until her Lawyer arrived. She waited no more than a few minutes when another woman arrived.

Bethany knew that keeping her waiting, even if it was for just a few minutes, was usually a calculated move to make her feel nervous but she was determined to remain calm and not rise to the bait. She reminded herself to take deep breaths while she was left alone, and distracted herself by reminiscing on all the wonderful holidays that she had taken and enjoyed. This always had the desired effect of making her feel less nervous and she felt she would be able to handle whatever they wanted to throw at her.

The woman identified herself as Mrs. Brown and Bethany stood to shake her proffered hand.

Mrs. Brown sat herself down behind the desk, intentionally keeping herself at arms-length from Bethany, with the desk in between, serving as a barrier to keep things on a firm and professional footing.

They sat silently opposite each other for a very brief moment and in that pause sat eyeing one another up.

Bethany noted that Mrs. Brown (if that was really her name) was smartly dressed in a matching navy skirt, which fell just above the knee and had a slit to the back. The matching jacket was well-fitted and the white blouse that had a collar forming a loose bow tie, dangling from it, completed the professional look she obviously wanted to convey. Bethany was sure that her suit was a one-off bespoke one and not a factory production of outfits manufactured specifically for clothes stores and judging by the area she had been led into, the woman must have held a higher position in the firm than the previous Lawyer she was dealing with. Mrs Brown wore very little make-up, or so it seemed, but when Bethany saw her close-up, she realised that she had lightly applied a toner on her face and the lipstick and eye-liner was very low key, so it gave the impression that she did not want to attract too much attention to herself, as she had other more pressing matters to deal with. She wore little jewellery, save for an expensive watch at her wrist and small pearl earrings which completed the appearance of one who was confident in her own skin.

Bethany could tell that the place she had been led into was probably just a spare room as it was sparsely furnished with a laptop and keyboard purchased on it and an A4 sized note pad with the firm's letter head at the top, lying idly on the desk. A pen lay beside it and it was obviously part of the stationary as it was also embossed with the firm`s name in gold. It looked as though the pen and pad had rarely been used as the angle of the sun coming into the room revealed a slight sprinkling of dust on it.

Mrs. Brown explained that the previous incumbent had unexpectedly left the firm due to ill health and because of the resulting upheaval, her paperwork had been lost, along with the case notes.

Bethany feigned surprise and sympathy at the same time and wished him well.

She was aware of the real truth and was determined to play along with their subterfuge.

Once again Bethany had to go over the steps leading to her dismissal and as she spoke, Mrs. Brown was making notes. In between Bethany`s explanations, accusations were hurled at her and once again Bethany felt as though she was being unnecessarily victimised. She was treated as though she was the party that had committed an offence and she realised that the plan was to intimidate her and to gain information from her that was not pertinent to the case. Nonetheless, she continued without appearing to be fazed.

It seemed to her that they were also trying to find a loophole in her case to prevent it from proceeding any further but Bethany was adamant that she would be able to supply the relevant facts of her dismissal.

Mrs.Brown must have assumed that Bethany no longer had any documents to support her case and her expression, when Bethany explained she had copies safely stored away, took her by surprise but she did not display it. It was only the twitch at the corner of her mouth that betrayed her astonishment by this disclosure.

Assuming that the interview was drawing to a close, as no more notes were being taken, Bethany was reminded to bring in all her paperwork to substantiate her claims.

After her treatment Bethany was tempted to take her case elsewhere and made it apparent. However, she was assured that the firm would pursue her case to its final outcome but they had wanted to ensure that her case was airtight and that there was nothing that she was holding back, hence their thorough interrogation. Bethany feigned consternation at the suggestion of her lack of co-operation and thereafter, was treated with some sympathy.

As the conversation continued, it seemed that Mrs. Brown was trying to stall her with repeated questions, following the same line, by which time Bethany became exasperated.

Another hour passed, during which time, she was offered some light refreshment and the conversation turned more relaxed and informal. The appointment finally drew to a close and Bethany was relieved to be walking out of the office, thankful that she had finally escaped. At one stage, she thought that they may hold her there against her will, so loathe were they to let her leave, but she realised it was just her imagination as she breathed a sigh of relief.

She headed back towards the safety and comfort of her home.

She was going to have to rethink her approach and

perhaps make her job search a priority now instead.

With this in mind she got into her car and headed home.

She remembered that she still had the bags full of clothes in the trunk of her car and she reminded herself to visit the charity shop the next day to donate them.

She was looking forward to a lovely cup of tea with some of the home-made biscuits she had baked earlier in the week and she pressed the foot on the gas pedal a little firmer, in her haste to get back home. As long as she kept to the speed limit, she was not concerned about driving a little faster, she thought to herself.

Chapter 11

She was not far from her house now and as she got closer to her street she could hear sirens in the distance and a fire truck was rapidly approaching as she glanced in her rear view mirror. She steered her car to the side of the road to let it pass and continued on towards home, praying to herself that whoever needed the assistance of the fire service would be unharmed. As she turned into her road there was a crowd gathering close to where she lived and a sudden feeling of dread came over her. Trying to ignore this she glanced in the direction of her house but the spectacle that she saw as she approached made the hairs on her arms stand up and once again she felt a cold chill pass down her spine.

She could not believe how adversely her fortunes had changed since meeting the stranger because staring straight ahead was a scene she hoped she would never have to witness.

The house that had been passed down to her by her parents who had died years earlier in a tragic road accident was now completely engulfed in flames and the fire brigade were working fiercely to bring the fire under control.

She had only last year revamped the kitchen and had the whole place re-wired and re-decorated, at the same time, so it was inconceivable that the wiring could be at fault. She had even made sure that she had switched off all the appliances as well as the television as she knew that she would be out for an undetermined period of time.

She parked her car away from the house and started

running towards it.

The fire crew now asked the gathering crowd to move back a safe distance and evacuated the neighbouring houses as the smoke was spreading as it started entering buildings either side of her house. Large flames were coming out of the roof of her house and the fire officers were finding it difficult to tackle the blaze as the force of the wind had begun to increase, changing direction at the same time.

Another truck now flew in to assist the other fire crews who were struggling to keep the fire under control and it appeared as though more homes would be engulfed in the flames. There was a flurry of activity as she saw the fire crews who had only moments ago entered the building now come rushing out of the house and suddenly there was a large explosion as the roof of her house caved in and the walls started collapsing.

For a moment there was stunned silence amongst the gathering crowds as they feared that someone may have been seriously injured inside whilst tackling the blaze but after a few moments it became clear that no-one had been hurt.

The police were now directing the crowd to move even further back for their own safety so that the whole area could be secured.

She tried breaking the cordon that had been set up moments earlier but the police would have none of it, immediately stopping anyone from passing. She shouted at them to allow her through because it was her house that was on fire.

Time seemed to stand still as the emergency services did

everything they could to make the area safe and after what felt like several hours but was probably only minutes later the fire had been completely extinguished. The tell-tale signs of the fire lingered in the air as a smell of burning hung in the air and a plume of smoke wafted up to the sky.

A mass of black ashes was all that was left of the house that once stood proud and the devastation Bethany felt was now complete. Everything she possessed save for the bags full of clothes, her laptop, some documents and her car had gone up in smoke. Photo-frames of her family, her parents and grand-parents, as a reminder of earlier happier days, had been destroyed and all that was left of them were the memories in her head, as she stood there in desolation and despair.

The only consolation was that although the fire had been intense there had been no loss of life and no other homes nearby had been affected but that was little comfort to her, at this moment, as she was the only person who had been affected by it.

She stood in front of the place that she had once called her home but now it was difficult to imagine that this ruin of rubble had once been a safe refuge which had offered her comfort and where she could rest her weary limbs. Once she stepped into the threshold she knew that she could close off the outside world for a short while and enjoy her own company but now she could enjoy no such pleasures.

As she observed the scene around her, large blackened uneven boulders were the only remnants of a house that once stood so proud and strong. Shattered blackened glass, was all that remained of the windows as they had scattered asunder in the explosion. She could see charred ashes as she stood at a safe distance, looking through the gaping holes of her house and emerging from the ground, were blackened brick edges, sticking out, like sharp knives waiting to cut deep if you got too close. It felt as though her life had been torn into shreds and the pieces laid down on the ground for all to see.

There was no meaning to this wanton destruction and she felt completely deflated, as though the wind had been taken out of the sails.

This house had been her sanctuary for so many years but now there was nowhere to go and no-one to turn to.

She suddenly felt all alone, exposed by the brutality of all this.

She didn`t know whether to laugh or to cry as she stood and gazed amongst this rubble of heap that was scattered all over the ground. It was a reflection of the turmoil within, her heart was broken into shreds and although an observer may have seen a beautiful woman with her tangled mass of hair tied back trying to make order in a world of disorder the eyes would have revealed a shocking sadness and emptiness, almost a glazed look that was seeing but not really seeing.

Bethany felt that she had been in a war-zone such was the numbness she now felt.

The crowd had long ago dispersed as the excitement of the situation had faded away for them and the police had taken away the cordons except for the area around her house which had orange tapes all around supported by rods dug deep into the ground to support the tape.

Fire inspectors were now in attendance trying to find clues as to how the fire had started but Bethany could not offer any answers as she had taken all the necessary precautions to avoid precisely this kind of situation, just as she usually did, whenever she left her house.

As she walked around the blackened ashes, kicking aside some of the rubble she was stopped in her tracks by a glistening piece of metal she must have exposed buried deep underneath. As she bent to pick it up, she realized it was her hand-held recorder which she often used to remind herself of important tasks or errands that needed to be done.

The whole thing was intact, somehow untainted by the fire.

She could not understand how it had remained undamaged.

Then she remembered that she had kept it in a fire-proof container, along with her keys and other important documents but she had taken those documents and keys with her and left the recorder in the empty box.

She hit the play button, merely to see if the device was working and not really expecting to hear anything.

To her amazement voices could be clearly heard on it and as she bought the recorder closer to her ears curious to hear what had been recorded, her whole body froze.

Two voices could be clearly heard conversing with one another.

She immediately recognized the voices even though there was some slight background noise, that sounded like crackling and the more she listened, the more she was certain that it was probably the sound of fire.

The voices were of the same two people, claiming to be police officers, who had interviewed her when she had tried to help the stranger but what they were doing in her house she wondered.

It was completely baffling.

Why would they be here of all places, in her house.

As she continued listening, their intentions became perfectly obvious.

One of them could clearly be heard shouting a word of warning to the other, in an urgent plea, to exit the house immediately. He had got carried away with dousing the house in an inflammable liquid and the flames were now moving faster than he had anticipated. She then heard the sound of metal clanging against metal followed by some more crackling sounds.

Then the other individual could be heard to swear in reply and then shout at his colleague at the same time, stating that he had found nothing incriminating in the house that would connect her with the stranger.

Their search had yielded nothing to link her with him, nor any documents regarding the legal case she was going to mount and then it was followed by a loud "whoosh" sound then some scrambling and muffled sounds and then the recording buzzed and crackled as the sound of the fire took hold of the house.

Upon hearing all this, Bethany understood why she had been delayed by all the unnecessary questioning and impeded in her wish to return home sooner.

She fumed in anger and grief.

Her whole life was now in ruins and it was no accident.

She now had incontrovertible proof, if any was needed,

that these people had intentionally caused the fire to her house and been responsible for her homelessness. To add insult to injury, they were also to blame for her losing her job.

She was determined to go to the authorities to explain the tragedy of the last few weeks and to alert them to the individuals responsible so that they could be punished.

No sooner had those thoughts arisen from her mind when the warning that the stranger had spoken to her now rang so true in her ears…"Don`t trust anyone" he had warned her.

Now, she had a clearer understanding about the truth of what he had said.

A myriad number of thoughts continued coursing through her mind and her head started spinning into even more confusion.

If she could trust no-one then she must hide the recorder before anyone witnessed her retrieving it, in the event that anyone was watching her.

She could not be sure that the two men had made their getaway and they could be watching from a distance, waiting to pounce on her again.

She no longer felt safe.

She discreetly placed the recorder in her pocket by taking out her handkerchief and pretending to sneeze, then carefully wrapped the recorder around it and started walking back towards her car. Before she had taken a few steps, someone tapped the back of her shoulder and she feared that her secret had been discovered.

Chapter 12

To her relief as she turned around, it was only her next door neighbour.

Although she did not know the lady very well they always kept a polite distance, exchanging pleasantries, whenever they met.

Bethany thought that she was a busy-body as she could often be seen surreptitiously lifting her net curtains in the front first floor room of her house every time Bethany left for work in the mornings. Bethany always felt as though her neighbor was spying on her because she was always at the window, when she left for work in the morning and when she returned late in the evening. It was one reason why Bethany would close her front door gently, on her way out, so as not to arouse her from awakening but she never succeeded. Her neighbour was always there, seemingly glued to the window.

It was as though her neighbour had a sixth sense, like dogs running to the door, wagging their tail and barking madly, so excited in anticipation of seeing their owners once again, having waited patiently for them to return home, only in this instance, Bethany was never glad to see her at the window.

She really did not want to exchange any pleasantries at this moment but she could not avoid her neighbour as she stood in front of her, blocking her progress.

Bethany stepped to one side to move away but her neighbour was determined to speak to her and caught hold of one of her arms, preventing her from escaping. She whispered to her as though not wanting to share her secret with anyone else and Bethany had to lean down slightly to bring her ear close towards her mouth and what she had to say to her stopped Bethany in her tracks, bringing her full attention on to her neighbour, at the same time.

The neighbour explained that she had seen strangers loitering outside her house moments before the fire and as she continued observing them discreetly behind the curtain of her upper bedroom window, she had watched how one of them stood as a lookout in front of Bethany's house, whilst the other had attempted to enter from the front door. The neighbour was sure that he had no key because he brought out a large thin metallic object that he had hidden inside his jacket and began to force his way, rather gingerly into the house. Just as he cracked open the door he then signaled, for his accomplice to enter.

As she was watching them breaking into the house, the neighbour went to grab her phone so that she could record their movements on it.

She rarely used these smartphones and struggled to work them out but after grappling with it for a few moments she found the record button and pressed it, zooming in on their movements and just in time to have a clear view of them as they entered the house.

As she stood waiting by the window for a few more moments there was no activity but she could imagine them going through the whole house searching for valuables so she stopped recording and immediately called the police, giving them a clear description of the men. It seemed an age, waiting for the police and she was sure that the intruders must have rummaged through the house from top to bottom in that time, taking away any of her valuable possessions they would have found. Her neighbour explained that she could not understand why it was taking the police so long to arrive and she was tempted to go outside and ring her doorbell, certain that it would stop them in their tracks and they would scarper.

However, she realized that if she interrupted them, then in their desperation to get away, they may attack her and she was a vulnerable old lady, so they would easily be able to overpower her, if she stood in their way, so she decided against it. It would do her no good if she was injured, or worse still killed so she refrained from going anywhere near the house.

Instead she stood hidden behind the curtain ready to record them leaving the property.

In no time at all, there then followed a flurry of activity outside. She pressed the record button once again, this time to see the two men scampering out of the front door as though they had seen a ghost. She thought that perhaps they had heard the police siren and was glad that they were finally coming but she could not hear it at all and was deeply disappointed to see no car approaching.

She was about to dial their number once again but then came the smell of badly burnt toast wafting from outside. She was certain that she had left nothing on in the oven and was about to head downstairs but as she turned her attention back out of the window, she caught something from the corner of her eye. She looked in the direction where her attention had been caught and she saw a plume of thin smoke coming from Bethany's house. Now she understood why they were in such a hurry to leave.

She immediately called the fire brigade, alerting them to what she had witnessed and as she waited for them she wondered why the police had still not arrived.

While she waited and waited, she explained to Bethany, that she was becoming very anxious, as plumes of smoke as well as flames, could now be seen raging from Bethany's house. A roaring blaze had taken hold now and she was sure that if the emergency services did not arrive soon there would be nothing left of Bethany`s house if the fire was left to continue burning out of control like this.

It was fortunate that the building was a detached property but she was concerned now, that the flames would fan out further into her property and engulf all the nearby properties too.

Her neighbour could not understand what was wrong because the emergency services were so slow to act. Now, even the fire brigade were not responding to her earlier calls and she was left anxious and worried as to why the calls were being ignored. After all, the fire station was very close by and so they should have arrived by now.

It was only after three repeated calls on her part, did the first fire engine finally pull up, at least a good twenty minutes after her initial call.

It was followed behind, by a police car. Her neighbour was quite astonished by these delays and she explained to Bethany that she had questioned the police officer who had pulled up in his car. He claimed not to have been notified of anything, until only a few minutes ago, when they were called by the fire services of a serious fire and hence their presence now.

Bethany became a little agitated upon hearing what her neighbour had just shared with her.

As she mentally processed all this information, she was left fuming and fearful at the same time.

She now understood the stranger's warning, imploring her not to get involved in his affairs.

He had told her to walk away from assisting him and to forget everything she had witnessed.

Now the repercussions of ignoring his pleas were apparent for her to see.

Her life may not have been in danger but all her possessions, her job, in fact everything that gave her security and all that she held dear had just gone up in smoke.

It was fortunate that there had been no casualties, she thought but that gave her little consolation at this moment.

She wanted to report these villains to the authorities but it appeared that they were complicit in all of this too. How else could she explain the intentional delays in salvaging her home and blocking her from apprehending the arsonists`.

If she could not trust the authorities then whom could she trust.

She had always associated the Police with being a positive force whose prime responsibility was to be neutral and enforce the rule of law in a balanced way but her own recent and personal experiences with them had started her questioning not just their true role in society but also the role of leaders in high places.

Were they a force for good or evil or were they in place to control and suppress citizens.

Did they expect the masses to follow the rules made up by them or by some despotic leader and his cronies, whose purpose was solely to satisfy their own personal desires and to maintain a firm control on that power, with the camouflaged excuse, to protect and serve society?

She had always been taught that the true reason that democracy flourished in the first place was to create prosperity so that everyone could share in that wealth but now those well-intentioned and altruistic principles had been abandoned for something that felt ominous and dangerous.

The unfair manner in which she had been treated by her own employers was a prime example of being made a scapegoat for some imaginary and made up transgression and now her faith in any type of Authority had raised so many questions that she was too scared to contemplate the unthinkable.

Perhaps it was better to bury her head in the sand and avoid confronting it because she already had so much to deal with and these kind of thoughts would just cloud the already muddied water in her brain and cause her endless mental anguish and suffering, with no positive outcome. It was best not to overthink this or jump to conclusions that would probably land her in even more muddy waters and so she decided to deal with the most pressing matter and leave that problem to those who would be better equipped to handle it. Let them stand up for the masses, she thought. She was just a minion in the whole scheme of things and her involvement would only attract more trouble to an already messy and complicated life.

As she pondered these questions she wondered if the intruders were still watching the scene from a distance, spying on her, just as surely as they had done, when she was on holiday.

She considered running away as far away as possible, from here so she could shut out her mind to all of these tumultuous events and turn her back on it.

She was sure, though, that that was precisely their intention, to scare her into submitting to her fears and raising a white flag, finally surrendering. However, she was certainly not broken yet and giving up was not in her DNA. Her parents had brought her up to be unshakeable when confronted with challenges and always encouraged her to face them head on, like a bull standing its ground in the face of provocation.

This was hardly the danger they would have envisaged her having to face.

Besides even if she did escape, there was nowhere for her to escape to and to make matters worse, she had nobody she could rely on.

How was she going to face this disaster, she asked herself.

As she stood there, forlornly gazing at this wanton destruction, her eyes began welling up with tears and before she could stop them, trickles of water started coursing down her cheeks.

She tried to stop herself and turned away, from her neighbour's hold on her arm pulling out a tissue from her pocket. She blew her nose loudly, and wiped away her tears. Waving a white flag like this would do her no good, she scolded herself as she fought back even more tears.

Her neighbour could see how visibly upset she was and invited her into her home to offer a comforting shoulder to cry on and a hot cup of tea to banish her worries.

It was silly how a cup of tea could provide all the answers, Bethany thought but she meekly accepted it as there was nothing else she could do at that moment.

It was the first time she had been invited in to her neighbour`s house and now was not the time to refuse. As she entered her neighbor`s threshold, there was a familiarity about it that she could not place.

Words were on the tip of her tongue but they would not form in her mouth and just a whispering gasp came out. She had been left utterly shocked and speechless by all that had just passed and now she just wanted to sit down and calm her throbbing head.

She let her neighbour guide her into the kitchen and sat meekly on the chair that was offered to her. As she looked around she startled herself by knowing the exact layout of the ground floor, even the kitchen table and chairs. She could not understand how it was possible to fathom all this when she had never entered her neighbor`s house but she was in no fit state to ask her anything about it just yet.

She accepted the tea and home-made vanilla cake that her neighbor placed on her plate, even though it was a little too sweet for her liking but she did not complain as it was a welcome relief as she began to feel a little calmer and more like herself.

There was a lot for her to digest, from the events her

neighbour had shared with her and for a moment she just wanted to enjoy the feeling of being looked after and comforted.

It reminded her of her mother who would soothe her whenever she fell down outside in the garden and came running into the house, squealing with the pain of the fall. As soon as she heard her mother's comforting tones and gentle hand on her she felt it all ease away.

How she wished she could run to her mother now and be lost in her embrace but there was no chance of that. Her parents had died years ago but the void they had left had never been filled and it was at times like this when she needed a shoulder to cry on that she really missed them both.

She rarely looked back into the past like this and wished that things were different but today for a brief second, she pitied herself and wondered why God had left her an orphan.

She was brought back to the present by her neighbour's gentle prodding as Bethany had not answered her.

Bethany's face was drained of all color despite the tea and cake she had just gulped down and her pale appearance just added to her neighbour's concern for her. It increased even more as a lack of a reply, or any words, for that matter on Bethany's part were convincing her that she needed medical attention, something that she was not equipped for.

As she stood to call for help, Bethany came out of her reverie and thanked the neighbour for her kindness and assured her that she was beginning to feel better, despite appearances.

If she could sit here for a while and gather her thoughts Bethany was sure she would return to normal, although what that meant, as she spoke those words, she was not sure.

Her neighbour let her sit there in silence for a while as she herself was uncertain as to what to say.

What words were there when one had lost their home moments before and parents` years before to add to that misery. She could find no words.

After what seemed like hours, but were only minutes, Bethany realized she had to start doing something if she was to find a place to stay.

It must have been as though her neighbour had read her mind because realizing that Bethany had nowhere to stay now, she suggested that Bethany stay with her for a few days until she could find herself a suitable place.

Bethany was taken aback by her kindness as she had only ever exchanged a few pleasantries with her, despite living so close and she could never imagine inviting a total stranger into her home. Nonetheless, she accepted her offer with gratitude and agreed that it would be for a short time.

She felt guilty now for labelling her a nosy neighbour and avoiding contact with her until this moment. Now her opinion of her instantly changed and she decided not to be so judgmental about people in the future. Her need to protect herself had caused her to become so insular and added to that, living on her own had merely added to this narrow-mindedness and she now realized that perhaps other people must have seen her as being off hand and selfish. Her blinkered view was partly because she had nobody to take care of but also because she did not want to be hurt ever again. The death of her mother, father and younger brother had been such a tragic event that she realized now that she still had some scars deep inside that needed healing.

Now looking at her neighbour she was grateful that she had been so inquisitive, otherwise she would never have discovered the truth of what had really happened to her home and she would have put it down to an unfortunate accident.

She decided to accept her neighbour`s kind offer on condition that Bethany pay for the time she stayed with her.

She wanted temporary relief from the stress of looking for a place to stay and concentrate on finding herself a job instead. At the same time, she could keep an eye on the progress of the investigation into her house fire and watch if either of the intruders had the audacity, to return to the scene of their crime. She doubted that they would but she could not be certain of anything anymore, and, if they did return, she would confront them in order to force a satisfactory answer to her predicament, which she was certain they were responsible for.

So she retrieved the bags full of clothes, that she had intended for donating to the charity shop, together with her laptop and documents from the car, parking it outside her neighbour`s driveway.

She was thankful that at least she had not taken the contents of the black bin bags to the charity shop yet. Some of those clothes would have to suffice now, as her new wardrobe. At some later stage she would sort through them once again and separate the ones that would no longer be of use and deposit them at the local charity. She was thankful no matter that the important documents such as her passport and driving license were still in her possession.

She intentionally avoided looking towards the devastation next door and focused on looking in front of her only, like the sharp focus of an arrow, not being deflected by anything or anyone.

She had to remain focused.

She had to concentrate on what to do next, not on what had passed as she would easily become deflated, which was understandable, considering these recent earth-shattering events.

There was a lot to do now and she wanted to keep herself busy, to stop her from feeling sorry for herself.

The first priority was to inform the insurance company about her present homeless situation and then wait for them to help her find accommodation.

Her job search would have to be put on hold, for the moment, and she would have to make allowances for these unforeseen circumstances.

After her neighbour had recounted how Bethany`s house had been destroyed, she asked her if she could take copies of the visual recordings she had made from her phone. She also did the same with her own voice recordings as she wanted to provide irrefutable evidence of the events that had transpired to the insurance company so that they could begin investigating her claims.

She was not sure that they seemed to understand the

gravity of the seriousness of what she had told them, when she called them but at the moment, that was not her concern. At least she had immediately notified them of the change in her circumstances, the rest was up to them to sort out, after all, wasn`t that what she paid her yearly premiums for.

When she had initially contacted the insurance company about her suspicions they were skeptical about her explanations and hinted that perhaps she was deflecting the blame away from herself, a common ruse amongst those committing insurance fraud. She was sure that this evidence would alleviate their doubts as to her guilt and would, if anything, point the investigation in the right direction and bring it to a speedier resolution. It was their one common goal, to bring the perpetrators to justice and bring an end to the matter and if she could do anything to hasten the process then she would do everything in her power to do whatever it took.

She was glad that at the last minute, during her appointment with the Employment Lawyer`s she had decided to take her laptop. In the eventuality, it made it easier for her to keep copies of the recordings and then transfer them onto a USB stick. She would ensure that she kept them in a safe place, where no-one would find them!

As she formed new files on her laptop, she remembered that she had stored some of her parents` pictures on her laptop, along with other happy memories she had shared with her grandparents. She never envisaged losing all her possessions in such a dramatic way but she was relieved now, that at least she had some evidence of her family`s existence because memories alone would not emotionally sustain her in the current situation she found herself in. At home before she went to sleep at night, she would look at their photos beside her bed, always saying a prayer, hoping they were happy, wherever they were.

In the last decade, with the wealth of her holiday experiences and extensive travel to some remote regions, she was certain that there was a life after death and hoped that her parents had taken rebirth, in a safe and beautiful place.

These were contrary to the beliefs that they had imposed upon her when they were alive but she firmly believed that ideas and beliefs needed to evolve in order to allow people to grow and learn because having a fixed mindset only limited one's expansion.

She wished she could bring back the days when her parents would sit with her discussing all the varied topics, from politics, ethics, philosophy and so much more. She missed the intellectual conversations she had shared with them and knew that they were trying to broaden her mind so that she would not be closeted and biased towards one view which would limit her outlook of life. They wanted her, above all, to be a generous spirited and open minded human being who only saw the best in everyone.

She felt that they would have been saddened to see how she had closeted herself, in recent years, choosing to remain content in the comfort and security of her employment and not really stretching herself. They had groomed her to be inquisitive and not to accept whatever she was told like a subservient slave, but rather, to question everything and draw her own conclusions. Now all of that was a distant memory and since they had died she had become completely transformed, so much so that they would not have recognized her. She had become an introverted person who was happy in her own company, closing her heart and mind to everything around her.

Perhaps one day this would change but right now this was what kept her safe and protected and she was not going to relinquish that approach any time soon.

The next few days whizzed by in a buzz of activity as she dealt with all the paperwork regarding her insurance claim.

The daily reminder of looking at the remnants of her house from out of the upstairs window of her neighbour`s house was a constant thorn in her mind, trying to bring emotions to the surface that she did not want to examine at the present time, so she kept them in check.

She knew she had to go there one day, even though the area had been cordoned off and notices put up, prohibiting anyone from entering. She wanted to take her own photographs to further substantiate her claims of suspected arson.

She had been keeping an eye out for anyone who dawdled around the property or showed an unnecessary interest in it.

Furthermore, she did not want anyone to contaminate the area or hide any evidence and she was sure that thus far, no-one had come to inspect the area in or around her crumbled house.

But at this present moment in time, she would stay away.

Chapter 13

After the buzz of activity the previous week, this week slowed down to a crawl, and the inactivity around her house made her feel exasperated by all the inaction so she took it upon herself to look around the remains of her house in search of any suspicious clues.

She could not understand why no-one had come to investigate the scene but she realized that it should not have come as a surprise to her. Something, or someone was working against her and she concluded that she would not sit back and accept the inaction but that she would act, even if it meant upsetting the current status quo.

She made her way past the cordons and moving around carefully, so as to disturb as little of the scene as possible, she started taking photographs, making sure that no-one was watching her.

She had worn gloves so as not to leave anything incriminating and she started clicking at random areas around the house. She forced herself to hold back the tears that were threatening to surface and become detached from the process, although it was not easy.

Once upon a time she took photographs of ruins like this, mercilessly carrying out instructions, for the insurance company she represented and now she realized how helpless the occupants of the destroyed houses must have felt, to lose everything in one fell swoop.

It was difficult for her to come to terms with and she was sure that many of them must have been left shell-shocked for a long time afterwards. She finished her task and took copies of the evidence and stored it away in the storage facility she had hired for such a purpose.

She then waited.

It was fortuitous, for her, that she had taken action because the very next day, a fire inspector arrived at the scene.

She had rushed out of her neighbour's house and from where she was positioned, she would have been unseen by anyone next door as there was a hedge separating her house, or what was left of her house and her neighbour's.

She had seen him moments ago, park his car close by and walk towards her "house" from the upstairs window. She had not intentionally been keeping an eye out but she had heard the slamming of a car door and was curious to see who it was. She was easily able to identify that the car belonged to the fire department, as emblazoned on the side of it in red bold letters were the words "Fire Inspection Services."

She was sure that she had been unseen and walked beyond the hedge towards the house and she was about to call out to him but the words stuck in her throat as she watched him surreptitiously remove items from the ground and pocket them into a hold-all that he had been carrying. He had been too busy in his undertaking to notice anyone watching him and he must have thought that he was unobserved, otherwise Bethany was sure he would not have removed anything from the scene.

As she approached him, the crunching noise under her feet alerted him to her presence. Without warning he immediately turned on her, threatening her and gesticulating towards her to immediately leave the scene, for trespassing.

Bethany's explanation that the house belonged to her fell on deaf ears and only served to aggravate him further. So she had no option but to retreat towards the cordon where she waited for him to finish.

As she stood watching him, she could not understand his reprimand. After all, she had never met him before and she had merely approached him to ask him how the investigation was progressing but he had stopped her from uttering another word.

He could see that she would not go away and so abandoned whatever he had come for and walked towards her.

She thought she had given him sufficient time to calm down by creating a distance between them and that he would now talk to her more civilly as she had abided by his request but how wrong she was.

As he approached her he told her, in no uncertain terms, that she was forbidden to go anywhere near her house and if she was ever discovered near there again, she would be reported to the authorities. They suspected her of being responsible for the blaze and her presence there would provide proof to them that she was intending to sabotage their efforts by interfering with the ongoing investigations.

Bethany was completely taken aback by that comment and could not believe what she was hearing as he turned his back, walked past her and strode away. He quickly rushed to his car threw the hold-all into the back seat, turned on the engine of the car and raced away without uttering another word or even glancing in her direction.

As Bethany stood there alone, her suspicions were aroused, when she realized that he had done nothing more after her entrance onto the scene. He had not even inspected the area to search for any clues as to the cause of the fire and she was certain that it was a dereliction of his duties to act in this manner.

She had once been a fire inspector herself and was aware of their roles and responsibilities and she wondered now, if he really was who he claimed to be.

He had failed to introduce himself when she had told him who she was and he had even tried to hide the hold-all he was but it was too bulky not to be noticed.

Despite driving a car that belonged to the Fire Services, she wondered now if it was stolen and decided that she would find out if they had sent a representative round to inspect the area.

As she trudged back to her neighbour's house, she realised that as soon as he had seen her, he had returned to his car in a rush, probably not wanting to be identified. Whatever he had picked up and placed in the hold-all would probably now never see the light of day and she was doubly glad that she had taken the photographs the day before.

He must have assumed that he had got away with removing the evidence but she had the images to prove otherwise and she would submit them to the insurance company to validate her claim.

Chapter 14

During the time that Bethany had been living with her neighbour she had become better acquainted with her and she was now used to being in Bethany's company. It had made them feel more comfortable to be around each other so her neighbour was able to open up to her.

She was a very independent woman, going to church every Sunday and volunteering there twice a week, usually Wednesday and Friday. She was in a good state of health and usually walked to the local park every day to ensure that she remained fit.

Bethany was surprised to hear this because she rarely saw her going outside but she would have been at work so that was probably the reason that she must have missed seeing her.

Her neighbour's house was in good order, everything in its place and although there was very little clutter, it did not feel empty. She cooked her own meals and was quite independent although she did have a cleaner who came once a week to do the dusting and hoovering. That was one task she could not undertake and Bethany understood why. It would take an hour or more, to cover the whole house from top to bottom and it was certainly no job for a woman of seventy. Especially when it involved lifting the vacuum cleaner upstairs and then down again. The hoover was quite a cumbersome machine and she could see it was quite an effort to drag it around.

Bethany knew how burdensome it felt, whenever she had to clean her own house and she had always wished that someone could do the cleaning for her too. However, as she was the only person living there it would be silly to ask for help as she was young and agile and could easily manage these mundane tasks herself.

As her neighbour got into conversation with Bethany, she had explained how her parents had moved into the property when Bethany was just a young child, probably no more than four or five years old. Her neighbour told Bethany how she had sometimes looked after her when her parents were sometimes indisposed. In her former years, Bethany recalled that they owned an antiques shop and her father would sometimes be called away on business and so her mother would leave Bethany with her neighbour during the day to manage the shop. Bethany was aware in the back of her mind that she had stayed in a stranger`s house and how welcomed she always felt. At the time her neighbour`s husband was still alive and they both treated her as though she were their own. They had children of their own, a son who had immigrated to Australia and a daughter, who had met and then married an American, whilst studying there so she had also gone to live abroad.

Bethany was like a breath of fresh air for the couple and whenever she was around they felt as though they had been given a new lease of life. She was energetic and lively but very well- behaved, except for one embarrassing habit.

As soon as Bethany stepped into the house she would run to the kitchen begging for an ice cream. It was not just any ice cream though. It was a multi-flavoured ice-lolly that they always kept in the freezer just for her because they knew it was her favourite. Bethany could not recollect all of the details but somewhere in her distant memory she recalled being in someone's house and eating an ice-lolly on a hot summer's day.

Her neighbour confirmed it was the only thing that would persuade Bethany to come inside and once there she did not mind staying for as long as necessary.

Whenever young Bethany entered their house she would run to the freezer, expecting to be given an ice-lolly, even pointing to the freezer, knowing full well where it was stored.

Of course her parents tried to dissuade her from behaving in this manner but her neighbour understood that Bethany was too young to clearly understand that it was rude to immediately walk in, without being invited and ask like that.

After being served the ice-lolly, Bethany was content, listening to the stories that her neighbour would read from the book that her parents had left and she would wait patiently until they arrived to pick her up.

She never missed her parents while they were away as she knew that they would always return and take her back home, so she would never cry whilst she was with the neighbour's.

The neighbor explained that as Bethany grew older, she liked to be outdoors more and more and so she would often be playing by herself outside in the garden. She was a bit of a tomboy and would climb the tree in the back garden and even climb back down unaided, even though it was quite tall. She was happy playing on her own and was better suited in her own company. That was not to say that she did not like playing with other children but there were very few children living close and within her neighborhood so she settled in her own company.

Her father even built her a tree house because she spent so much time up the tree and it was always a challenge for her to come back indoors and her neighbour remembered how she had to be coaxed to come back inside, even when it was raining or cold. Bethany loved being outside in all weathers, as long as she was well wrapped and that had not changed to this day.

As the days passed, Bethany did not want to impose on her neighbour longer than was necessary so she had desperately been searching for a B&B, a temporary arrangement until her insurance claim came through but so far nothing suitable had come up. She knew she could not live with her neighbor indefinitely as they both needed to get back to living their own lives.

She had tried to remain upbeat about finding somewhere to stay and diverted her search for rented accommodation instead. Still no matter how many places she viewed, there was still nothing that had adequately met her needs; the rooms were either too small or she would have to share the bathroom with other tenants and that was one thing she could not face. Above all else she valued her privacy, especially more so after everything that she had been through. Some of the rooms she was shown were on the fifth floor where there were no lifts and she knew that trying to get furniture up the steps was going to be challenging as she did not know who to call on for assistance and she certainly could never manage this on her own. Some of the accommodation reminded her of her student days at University, when money was tight.

She had settled for the very basics then, as she was determined not to ask her parents for any handouts. She had saved enough to pay her way through University, which included rent for the three years that she had planned to be there for. Her first year was at the University campus where she was fortunate to have her own room which she furnished with a small bed, a Work-desk and a chair. If she was up early or had no lectures she would sometimes study at her desk, where she kept her laptop and some books. Other facilities, like the kitchen and bathroom were shared with three other University students who were studying different degrees to hers so she rarely saw them. This did not bother her as in those early days as she was less interested in socialising, and more intent on achieving good grades so that her parents would be proud of her as she was the first generation of her family to go to University. When the weather permitted she loved to be outdoors and joined study groups out in the open and she had fond memories of the friendships she formed whilst there, especially during her final year.

That was a long time ago and Bethany was not willing to make those sacrifices now at this time. After all, she had worked hard since her parents' unexpected and premature death, and she had become used to a certain standard of living, not necessarily a luxurious lifestyle but certainly one that afforded her some minor comforts. No matter how long it would take she refused to settle for anything less than what she had worked so hard for and continued on her quest for a temporary but suitable place to stay.

The insurance claim seemed to be going at a snail's pace and so Bethany decided to ask for her neighbour's assistance as she had no influence on the outcome. She was a neutral party and her neighbour's input would deflect any suspicions away from her and help clear up any confusion. Her neighbour had witnessed the two men entering her property and causing the fire so she could report that to the insurance company who would then, hopefully, change tack and not be so aggressive with her. So she asked her neighbour to contact them with the recording she had made showing the intruders entering Bethany's house illegally. Bethany asked her to inform them that it was the only recording she had of the incident because she was concerned of her involvement with Bethany. She wanted to ensure that her neighbour would remain safe, just in case they decided to turn on her as well.

Bethany had already experienced so much bad fortune, that she did not feel it would serve any purpose and was loathe to disclose to her neighbor, the circumstances which had led to her current predicament. If anything untoward did occur Bethany was ready to vacate the property at short notice but she was quite sure that they would not threaten an innocent old lady.

However, this could not be further from the truth.

Chapter 15

After her neighbour had given a statement to Bethany`s insurance company, Bethany hoped that things would now be processed more speedily and everything could be settled so that she could move on.

This was not to be.

A few days after her neighbour had contacted the Insurance Company, she was visited by two men claiming to be from there. They wanted to speak to her in more detail about what she had told them and after allowing them into her house, they settled down into the front room to have a chat. After some pleasantries were exchanged, they began to badger her about the truthfulness of the evidence she had submitted to the Insurance Company. Her neighbour was quite taken aback by their accusations and as the conversation progressed it became clearer to her that they were not there on behalf of the insurance company and begun to suspect their motives. She asked them to leave but they only continued pestering her even more. She had taken all she could and threatened to call the police but to her astonishment they reacted by threatening her and finally walked out, informing her, in no uncertain terms that if she continued to make the claim about the break-in and lack of co-operation from the insurance company in order to substantiate Bethany`s claims, her house would suffer the same fate as Bethany`s. The finality of their threat was made abundantly clear, as they slammed the door shut to her house with such force, that it made her jump and the house vibrate with it.

Their next act was even more brazen as they slid a box of matches into her letter-box, leaving little to the imagination.

Unfortunately, Bethany had been out, trying to find a place to stay and when she returned she found her neighbor in tears, shaking in distress at what had occurred.

In between the tears and shaking Bethany discovered what had happened and immediately decided to leave.

The old lady had been so kind in her hour of need but Bethany would not be responsible for jeopardizing the old lady's safety in return for a safe place to stay.

Bethany made her a cup of tea and assured the old lady that the same fate would not befall her as Bethany would not allow her to be placed in such a compromising position. Bethany thanked her profusely and explained to her that she had just found somewhere else to stay that day and would not impose any further on her hospitality.

Her neighbour suspected that Bethany was only trying to comfort her and was not being honest and so tried to dissuade Bethany from leaving, but in her heart, she knew that this was the only solution that would keep her safe. She was going to be left alone once again and she would miss having someone in the house to talk to but at the same time, she realised that there was nothing more she could do for Bethany. With a heavy heart she accepted Bethany's decision and asked her to stay in touch.

As Bethany started putting the scant belongings into her car, she could not help thinking about her homelessness situation once again and the despair she felt at having to leave so suddenly.

She knew that her leaving was inevitable one day but had not envisaged it being so sudden and so forced, nevertheless, it was the best course of action under the circumstances and she put on a brave face as she said her goodbyes. She promised that she would be in touch once it was safe to do so and for the moment she would leave no forwarding address with her neighbour as it was best that her neighbor did not know her whereabouts.

In truth Bethany`s search for a place to stay had been fruitless so far so she decided to widen the search of possible areas.

She recalled when she was very young, perhaps six or seven years of age, living with her parents in rented accommodation, whilst their house was being renovated.

The house had been handed down three generations and was in need of modernisation and so they had emptied it completely to make way for the builders to work their magic. Electrical and plumbing alterations were required and so the complete overhaul was going to take six months as they were also extending one storey out to the rear, to make way for a bigger kitchen.

She was so young and saw it as a wonderful adventure, then, but she could not imagine how stressful her parents must have found it as they both worked full-time then. Although her father had his own antiques business, it still required his full attention and the same applied to her mother. She remembered coming with them to view the progress and walking around the empty shell of the building every weekend. The house had served as a playground then and she was able to run around every nook and cranny, sometimes hiding away to play hide and seek with her parents. She knew that they pretended not to know where she was until, finally giving up her secret hideaway, she revealed herself. A smile emerged from her lips as those fond memories came dancing back.

As the memories came flooding back she also recalled staying with her neighbour`s, who looked after her, while her parents went looking for appliances and units for both the bathroom and kitchen. Even the lounge and dining areas in their house had to be refurnished and repainted, whilst the old dark-coloured wallpaper in most of the rooms had been stripped back to reveal walls that needed to be plastered and then covered by soft pastel paints which made the transformation in the house so final that it was like walking into a new house altogether.

The modernisation in the house meant that she now had her own large bedroom, complete with wardrobes that she no longer shared with anyone else. It only served to be more spacious as she still had the same amount of clothes as before but with more room. She was given her own mirror and dressing table and every time she sat down on it to brush her hair she felt like a grown-up. Countless times she had watched her mother stroking her hair and brushing away the tangles and now she was able to do the same with her own hair, only in her own bedroom.

She had been standing at the entrance of a B&B she had come to view and her mind was jolted back to the present by the owner who had answered the doorbell and asked her if she had come to view the room.

Bethany had driven here after phoning ahead and

arranging a time to view the place and she must have looked a sight standing there with her tousled hair and no make-up but there had been no time to spruce herself up after leaving so unexpectedly.

The owner of the B&B must have seen all sorts of people coming through her door so she made no comment as she allowed Bethany in. After being shown around upstairs Bethany decided to take up the offer of staying there for two weeks, with a possible further week added if she had found nowhere else by then.

Her room was neat and tidy and as well as the dining area, which served meals in the morning and evening there was also a lounge that overlooked a beautiful but small garden. It was covered in a well mown lawn, with bordered flowers and a bird fountain in the middle. As she gazed out, she could see two robins splashing around in the water, throwing it at each other, frolicking about for a moment, before flying off. This sealed her decision as she loved being in nature or observing how different creatures behaved with such unbridled joy and freedom. It was an emotion that had become very alien to her recently and looking out into the garden would blunt some of the pain she was going through right now.

It helped that the owner of the B&B was very friendly and easy to get on with and she had not been too inquisitive about Bethany's circumstances. She had been happy to accept Bethany's explanation of moving back to the area after a prolonged absence due to work commitments elsewhere. Bethany had gone on to explain that the area suited her as there was sufficient parking outside and it was close to the underground station, within two travel zones of Central London.

After paying the owner two weeks in advance with the option of adding another week, she unloaded one of the suitcases from her car and made her way to her room. She had bought three suitcases for the clothes that had been initially intended for the charity shop but which would now have to be used as daily wear for her as she had no other belongings after the fire. She was glad that she had arranged them into matching pairs of skirts, tops and shoes, and along with her trainers there was no need to take out the other bags at the moment. She thought it best not to take out all three suitcases out at once, as she did not want anyone questioning her as to why she had so many bags. At least the suitcases would look more presentable instead of the black bin bags she had put her spare clothes in before.

After finding her way around and locating the nearest local café`s, restaurants and shops Bethany began her search for a job. She had been to London and left her CV`s with the employment agencies and given her burnt out home as her current address. She knew that they would not know about the fire at the moment, as companies only confirmed the address through the Voter`s Roll register and hers had not altered, despite the fire. She had time to change it at a later date so she was not concerned with this piece of misinformation.

Bethany had not wanted to burden the owner of the B&B with any more of her circumstances than was necessary and so she avoided contact with her by being out every morning after breakfast and not returning until the early part of the evening, by which time she was so exhausted that she would give her a cursory hello before plodding upstairs to bed.

She had settled into a routine of visiting the employment agencies after breakfast every day and had repeatedly been informed that she would be receiving job offers in the near future and to be patient as all the formalities would take a little time.

She felt that her life had turned in an unexpected way, just when she thought she knew where it was heading, she had suddenly been jolted by a huge earthquake and caught in a whirlwind at the same time where the initial events had seemed so insignificant at first but now had become so great that she felt she had no control over them. Their reverberations were still being felt and she no longer had any control of where her life was heading.

Each day, as she waited expectantly for some news about her search for employment she was tempted to go back to her old house, just to prove to herself that what had really happened was not a dream but part of her current reality, as she still had great difficulty in accepting her present situation.

Finally, one day, unable to resist the temptation, as she was driving within close proximity of her house, she turned into her road to have a quick look. As she passed the ruins of her house she drove swiftly past, deciding not to stop and averting her gaze instead, knowing that if she stopped at where her house stood before, she would lose all her composure and probably break down in tears again at the sight of the burnt out ruins which were now protected by steel fences on all four sides. Glancing at the row of houses opposite her own that she once identified so closely with, especially whenever she left or returned home from work, she remembered feeling a sense of security and gratitude that she lived in a quiet and pretty residential street, with tree-lined pathways and hedges where she often heard birds chirping away from dawn to dusk, and where there was nothing to threaten the daily routine of life. She especially looked forward to hearing the twittering of the birds on the trees that she could see when alighting at her stop from the train. It gave her a welcome relief from the constant and busy chatter of office workers, with its constantly and irritating ringing telephones together with the ear-wrenching noise of the wheels of the train on the track, as the train came juddering to a halt at each of the twelve stops that took her home. She loved to view the greenery from her elevated position as she walked past the platform which overlooked a football field that always seemed to be deserted. The scenery always bought her back to a sense of calmness and tranquillity, after a heavy and stressful working day. The local council had long ago demolished the derelict buildings that once stood there and, where once, there had been posh high-rise offices standing proud and erect in the skyline, one by one, they had been vacated so that in their final years, they lay empty and abandoned, forgotten, like discarded pensioners whose usefulness to society no longer of any importance, so left to be ignored and neglected. Many years later, a property developer had bought and then immediately sold the land at an inflated price, to a major league football club, who had submitted plans to build a massive stadium to accommodate their large fan-base. The unsightly monstrosity, in the middle of a heavily built residential area was like putting the cat amongst the pigeons and the residents stood up in arms, fighting back as one unit. Where previously there had been discord and conflict, causing division and mistrust, now they worked together, with one main objective, to throw out the interloper. It was bad enough that years earlier, a few hundred yards further down, the council had given permission to build a school in place of the community playing fields that had been in existence for many years and which the public and smaller football clubs had used as their only means of recreation. This unwelcome and unexpected decision was the straw that broke the camel's back and the residents came out fighting. After several vociferous demonstrations and objections the plans were downgraded to one that was more amenable to both parties. A local gym and small leisure centre had been added to cushion the blow of an unsightly building in the middle of a dense residential area which local people could also access. The major league club had succumbed to the voice of the people, knowing that the bad press would only damage their reputation and bowed out ignominiously redirecting their focus elsewhere. The ground was given over to the local football club instead, who used it during the weekends for matches and the adjacent training ground, when not used by the players, was shared by residents who could arrange impromptu matches with friends.

As she recalled how she, her parents and the local community had banded together and got involved with the demonstrations, a trickle of salty water fell onto her face as the thought of that togetherness and bond that they had once shared had now disappeared. That common brotherhood and unity that she had taken for granted was a far cry from where she was now and it made her feel even more alone and abandoned than ever before.

Her regular commute and going to work was a routine that had become a part of her life and she could not understand how it had all kept her sane as all the memories came flooding back once again and more tears fell onto her face. She would walk down the flight of twenty two steps as she came down the stairs from the platform, even remembering that she would count the exact number of steps she had to climb down, and then displaying her ticket at the automatic turnstile as she came out of the station, she would walk past the parade of shops and then as they ended, turning right to enter her road. The telephone box at the corner and the entrance to the flats above the parade of shops were a familiar landmark to tell her she was close to home. As she continued walking along she would have to pass the two mini roundabouts that were positioned in such a way, as to divide the whole road, forming an obstacle that forced the cars to slow down, deterring them from travelling at break-neck speeds. Nonetheless, some drivers still used it as a race track, especially in the late and early hours of the day when traffic was almost non-existent. As she passed the tightly built row of houses she was always reminded that she was almost home and after a long and tiring day the sight of them bought a sigh of relief from her, thankful that another day was over and that she could now relax at home and be left to her own devices and do as she pleased, without having to think about any-one else.

She remembered thinking every time she approached this set of houses, how some surveyor must have got his measurements all wrong when he was spacing the houses on this street because all the houses except for this row had their own garages. He must have had to fill a large void because none of these houses had garages and they were built quite close to each other in comparison to all the other houses on this street and as a result, it seemed to set them apart.

She was not sure why she had driven there but she realised now that it was a mistake as the memories were too fresh and each one was opening an already raw and painful wound that was cutting deeper and deeper like a knife being forced in. She could not keep her emotions in check as she did not know how to deal with them and so she turned the car away, and made her way back to where she was presently staying.

She had just wanted to turn the clock back and forget about everything that had happened and be back in her house, safe and warm, cossetted from the outside world but she realised that she could never go back now, only forward and the tears started welling up as she parked her car in front of the B&B.

Recently, she felt morose like this, with no apparent reason, tears would fall unchecked from her face and as before, she let them continue until the emotions ran out of fuel. As the days flew by her inner turmoil continued unabated. It had now been weeks since the fire and she had heard nothing from the fire services or the Insurance firm.

After making enquiries, she had been informed that it would still take a further two weeks to investigate and they would notify her of the outcome if she would give them her forwarding address but Bethany refused to give this to them and instead made excuses, that she was moving from one place to another, and so, at present had no fixed abode. After all her experiences she felt it wise to give as little information away as possible and said that she would contact them instead. So until the matter was sorted, she was forced to stay in temporary accommodation for the time being.

At least she felt safe in the knowledge, knowing that nobody knew where she was staying and she even took precautions to ensure that it stayed that way by taking detours back to her place careful she was not being followed.

Three weeks passed with no progress and her stay at the B&B was drawing to an end.

She decided, on a whim, she would give herself a temporary reprieve and stay for a week by the coast in a Bed and Breakfast.

In view of her brittle state she was hoping that it would lift her ailing spirits.

In the past, the sound of water and the sea breeze always gave her a welcome relief from all her sadness and she hoped that it would have the same effect on her now. She was only a few hours' drive from there and so she informed the owner of the B&B that she would return in a week and even paid her in advance to show her sincerity and the owner accepted it without question.

Bethany gave her no indication of where she would be going in the meantime and she was certain that the owner was used to these comings and goings because she asked no questions.

Bethany drove towards the coast without taking a break, impatient to get there, now that she had made up her mind to go. Once again it was a B&B she had booked in advance with all the facilities close by as well as a small car park at the rear. There were hills overlooking the car park and a few miles further down was the coastline so she could easily walk there and back. The proximity of the sea was the main reason she had chosen this place and as she checked in and dropped her suitcase onto the floor of her room she sat on the bed with a huge sigh of relief, unable to believe that she had taken the courage to interrupt her job search to have this short break. As she sat there with her legs poised at the edge of the bed she looked around the room and her eyes stopped at the window where she could see views of the ocean. From here it looked like a blue veil had been laid down on the floor as it stretched beyond the visible eye and way beyond into the distant horizon. The skies matched the colour of the sea and if it was not for the boats in the distance with their unfurled sails, it otherwise appeared as one.

Her gaze stayed on this picturesque view and without realising it her body completely relaxed and she fell onto the bed and closed her eyes, intending to catch a short snooze.

Instead her sleep was interrupted as her stomach started

making grumbling noises, informing her that it was time to eat. She rose to her feet in panic and for a moment lost her bearings….where was she, how had she got here….the feeling subsided as she realised where she was and she slowly sat up on the bed, deciding what to do next.

She had just left her suitcase on the floor so she took out her face towel and after washing her face dried herself and made herself presentable before going downstairs to become better acquainted with her surroundings.

After a short stroll she returned to the B&B and sat for dinner. She had already made provisions for it for the first day when she had booked the accommodation and was glad now that she did not have to worry about food today. After a hearty meal decided she would go out for a longer walk beside the sea, hoping the fresh air would give her a god night`s sleep. When she was on holiday it always helped her to sleep well and today was no different. She waited for the sun to set as she loved to see the reflections of the last rays on the sea and returned to her B&B.

The week was spent swimming, walking, having massages and eating. She refused to look at a newspaper or watch T.V. and closed herself off from the outside world, apart from the solitary walks. She met very few people and apart from casual conversations with the owner of this B&B it was as though she had cut herself off and gone into solitary confinement. It suited her to not have to explain herself to anyone or make conversation and she could feel the tenseness in her body unwind and her mind beginning to gain more clarity.

Her uncertain future had been a major concern for her but for the moment, she would force all that to the back of her mind and surrender to the peace and tranquillity of her present surroundings.

She would take the opportunity to recharge her batteries this week and allow her mind to relax and switch off to everything that had contributed to turning her world upside down.

When the time came to face that situation she would but for now she would make the most of where she was.

She understood, a little now, why people went on pilgrimages. The silence on the outside penetrated their inner worlds giving them new insights and a resurgence that could not be gained anywhere else. That temporary escape gave time to put life on hold and to recalibrate it into a more joyful experience.

She even spoilt herself further by sitting outside a café, drinking tea and watching the world go by every morning, before taking her walks. She had always promised herself that she would do this and there was no better time than the present to finally give in to that desire.

That was one of the reasons she had decided to step outside of the conundrum of life and take a breather and as the week drew to a close she wished she could stay here indefinitely, but like her holidays in the past, it was time to face the outside world.

She made her way back to her temporary address at the B&B and she continued her search for a job with a little more gusto.

She had decided that finding employment was better

than asking for handouts.

After all her family had never applied for benefits as they were too independent minded to rely on the state and she was not going to start now. Even during the war when her grandparents had endured extreme hardships she remembered that they had just bitten the bullet and done whatever it took to improve their status and that attitude had been handed down to her parents and then to her so that she was not afraid to roll up her sleeves and do what needed to be done to get back to earning and supporting herself.

Now that she looked back at her forefathers, she was grateful that they had instilled this in her as she was sure that any other person who had suffered what she had in the last month would have easily wilted and just given up but she was made of much sterner stuff.

As it was a very pleasant day she decided to take a detour, taking a longer route to walk, than normal. She wanted to make the most of the sun that had managed to plot its way through the clouds and it felt a welcome respite after the spell of heavy rains they had experienced in the last few weeks which had caused some localised flooding. There was the inevitable public transport logjams, as some of the roads had been adversely affected by the flooding and she had heard on the radio that a few of them had even had to be closed down.

As a result some of the buses were on diversions and she did not want to face standing in queues and experience all the pushing and shoving that normally followed when transport systems broke down because it seemed that at this time, the worst side of peoples` characters were exposed. Their impatience and intolerance for one another always became heightened when something out of the normal routine upset the applecart. She had witnessed plenty of this whilst she was working, and she realised now, that she herself was once part of that hustle and bustle too. Being trapped inside a metal box, like cattle being prepared for slaughter had once been something she had accepted previously as part of her normal life and now, when she had the choice to avoid being entangled in that jostling, it came as a relief to her and she wondered how she had previously done it without question. If people had no other choice and were forced to do certain things, she reflected, they would feel compelled to do it, without question, just as she once had.

It was fortunate that the owner of the B&B had a habit of switching on the radio as soon as she was up and about as this was one way that Bethany was able to remain well informed with what was happening in the world. Otherwise Bethany would have been oblivious to the goings on outside of her sphere.

When she was living on her own she preferred the peace and quiet of the morning as it allowed her to think more clearly and it was a habit that she had grown used to. She found that she was able to easily find a way through any problems, after a good night`s sleep. She had read somewhere that the subconscious part of the brain started to kick in during sleep when the conscious part of the brain would "take a rest" and it was the reason why most people could find the clearing in the fog and find a resolution to any problem that they faced and she was no different. She just needed the extra solitude to face the world with more courage.

However, now, under these new circumstances she had to grow accustomed to the changes that were forced upon her and she realised it was best to accept the situation that she found herself in, rather than to fight it. Fighting drained her of energy and she needed to conserve it right now, as it allowed her to think with more clarity and focus. She needed that clear thinking now, more so, than at any other time in her life, as it sustained her through the dark days.

She noticed as she was walking how the weather was a reflection of her state of mind, a feeling of despair a few days ago when it had been overcast and cloudy, then thunderstorms and heavy downpours bringing a release of tears, which had now turned into optimism and relief now that the sun was out. It was funny how the weather seemed to be influencing her moods lately, ever since that encounter with that stranger, she thought. He had so much to answer for and if she ever met him again, which she seriously doubted, she would tell him as much.

So it was in this setting that Bethany found herself walking along the roads that she was not very familiar with. In fact, it was a new sensation even to be walking so much. She normally used Public Transport, either buses or the underground, and then walked the short distance to her office but today she had decided to walk from the Bed and Breakfast, towards the direction in which she previously worked.

She automatically put one foot in front of the other and it was as though her legs had a will of their own taking her somewhere, anywhere, away from the reminder that she was now homeless and no longer had a permanent place to live. She must have been walking for some time as she turned into a road where all the houses looked the same, imposing white-walled mansions with large steps leading up to the entrance with towering pillars at each side and black double doors standing so loftily, barring entrance to any unwelcome strangers.

Each of these mansions was protected by six foot enclosed iron-clad see through gates fronted by well-manicured lawns and colourful shrubs and borders with gravelled paths leading to the front entrance. Their white-walled buildings rose to the sky, creating a picture of perfection, like the buildings in Crete, their white painted walls accentuated by the backdrop of the blue azure skies and calm, still seas. She had the impression that the occupants were safely guarded and ensconced in their own homes, purposefully creating a barrier between themselves and the outside world, so that no-one was able to enter their threshold, without their express permission. The houses were set so far back that the front could easily accommodate several blocks of housing and there would still be room for garages. In this world of homelessness and lack of sufficient housing she wondered how these people could live with themselves. On the one hand, they displayed their wealth for all to see and yet on the other hand, they wanted to keep themselves hidden from the rest of the world in a way she could not imagine.

How fortunate, these people living in these expensive mansions must be she thought, not having to worry about where the next plate of food was going to come from or how they were going to cope with keeping a roof over their heads without the worry of bailiffs knocking at the door, summoned there, to collect arrears any way that they could. It seemed that only the mega-rich were immune to austerity and to the hardship of other people around them.

She was unsure where all this negativity and self-pity was emanating from as she had never felt like this before. Since her parents death she had not addressed the emotions that had been supressed for so long and perhaps now they were giving full vent in this manner. That was perhaps why this side of her character felt so alien to her and she could feel some anger and frustration building up, towards the world, for her present circumstances but she could not afford to be so negative and so put all febrile thoughts like this to the back of her mind. It would not help her current situation and, if anything, she would just dig herself into a bottomless dark pit that would consume all of her energy. To come out of it would take so much out of her that it was better to not put her mind in that place so she tried to concentrate on the present instead and take one step at a time. She realised that at some near future those emotions would have to be given the space to be voiced because otherwise, if they were kept in check, her body would begin to react physically, attacking her inwardly if she could not express the emotions outwardly and it would be to her detriment.

Approaching a bridge, she was distracted by the sound of the running stream beneath it and she stopped to look over the bridge. Her attention was caught by two white swans curled up close together at the edge of the river, on a narrow ledge where the sun's rays hit the ground, precisely in the place where they sat. It looked as though they were sunbathing in the midday sun at the height of summer basking in the rare warmth of their surroundings, canoodling at the same time as their beaks touched each other's. Nearby, a raft of mandarin ducks were gliding in the water, ducking their heads under the surface then coming up for air and then repeating the same movement again and again as she watched. It seemed as though they were trying to cool themselves down in this heat. From where she was standing, she noticed that they had positioned themselves in the shape of an arrowhead, each one dancing to a tune, but in unison. They would steady themselves from the strongly flowing undercurrents, their feet below the surface of the water seen to be wading furiously against the tide and then together ducking their heads into the water. She then saw why their heads were ducking so frantically in the water, to catch some food that passers-by had thrown at them.

She laughed quietly to herself because the scene she was presented with looked as though it had been orchestrated just for her, as though mother-nature was telling her to keep her head above water. She wished she had a camera to record this scene because no-one would have believed it if she had told them about it. As the stream meandered around a corner she noticed bluebells growing at the side of the river where it converged with grass overhanging from the edges. The blue bells stood very tall and they in turn were surrounded by orange and red flowers, as though forming a protection, for the fragile flowers that were being blown around by the gentle breeze. The sun's rays were reflecting on the river stream, causing it to shimmer in silver strips and she wished she could stand like this forever because the peace that she had craved for, was now in front of her at this precise moment.

She was reminded about her accidental meeting with the stranger and the subsequent tumultuous events that had followed and she remembered that she had other things on her mind that needed her attention. She did not have the time to stand and admire the view for too long. As if reading her mind, a crowd of tourists were approaching from the other end of the bridge, chattering loudly amongst themselves and that was her cue to move as she did not want to be drawn into the large crowd that was now coming towards her. She craved the temporary peace that she had just enjoyed and that had been lacking, for what seemed a very long time and she wanted to make the most of these few moments of lightness, so she paused there to take in the picture for just a few moments longer.

The crowd was drawing closer and their attention was diverted to the ducks who had started wading in their direction hoping for a morsel to eat.

Delighted with these creatures, and like an orchestra taking up their instruments in unison at that very moment, the tourists started pointing their cameras at the scene below, clicking with their cameras as the ducks who had now inadvertently formed a circle, began wading furiously closer and closer to them. The ducks continued waiting expectantly for a morsel from the crowd, angling their beaks up towards the air, and finally some of the people in the crowd obliged, throwing tiny morsels in their direction. The ducks greedily picked off the tiny bits and waited in the hope that more would follow but the crowd had grown tired and started walking away.

Bethany was completely entranced by the scene but was woken out of her reverie by the gathering noise of the crowds as they huddled together, and spoke even more animatedly, trying to decide where to go next.

Before they came her way and obstructed her path, she turned to walk past the bridge and followed the road as it meandered towards the shops.

She had taken this part of the route to work for so many years, that it was like second nature to her as she remembered all the road signs and the different shapes of the buildings that she passed on her way. Some of the buildings rose up so high in the sky, not quite as high as the skyscrapers that now loomed up in city areas but high enough to demand attention. She knew that many of them housed open planned offices that were the current trend in building design and she missed working in smaller closed spaces as they gave an element of privacy and seclusion at the same time. It suddenly dawned upon her that she no longer had to worry about where she worked, or office politics and all that went with it, for that matter, as she was not currently working. She chided herself for continuing to recollect her past as it was bringing up too many painful memories. She should start living now, in the present she reminded herself once again, as she constantly did throughout the day, and tried to forget about everything that had passed.

As she forced herself to come back to the present she realised that she had taken this route because she wanted to feel some form of normality, a reminder of how her life once was, it had become a habit for her going to work, coming home, going to work, coming home and the repetition of that routine was like a warm blanket, there when needed but discarded when too hot and she could not accept or even admit to herself that she was no longer working, had no home to go to and had no-one she could turn to for help. Here she was again thinking about the past.

As she walked past the building where she once worked she realised that she was subconsciously hoping to bump into her ex-boss at any moment and that he would tell her that her sacking had all been a mistake. If she could accept their mistake she could return to work as she was one of only a few reliable people in the firm and they would gladly have her back.

If she was truthful she knew this would never happen, she was living in a day-dream and she could not afford to allow herself that pleasure.

As she continued walking she found herself in front of the same café she went into before work where she would have a cafe latte to give her that caffeine trip she so craved before facing the daily grind like so many other people. Today, however she just walked past it and felt sorry for the people forming an orderly queue, like drug addicts waiting for their daily fix, but instead of drugs, it was caffeine giving them the "high" that they so desperately craved. She quickly walked past all the high street shops, ignoring the mannequins wearing the latest outfits and shoes, knowing that in the past, she was easily drawn into them, tempted to buy one or other outfit. Now that she had no excuse to go in she realised that she did not need so many pairs of shoes or outfits, anyway.

Perhaps the fire was the one good outcome after all. She would no longer spend her money needlessly on clothes that she would only wear once before being discarded.

Once upon a time she would have rushed to eat her lunch just so that she could go out to buy these clothes. All in the name of fashion, and an insatiable desire to buy, buy and buy, with no real purpose but to remain in tune with the current trends and some unsatisfied need within. It was almost like an addiction and the outfits in her cupboard bore witness to that. Some of them had never seen the light of day once she had bought them and they just hung there with the labels still stuck on them waiting for the opportunity to be admired but that day never came. Then she remembered, she no longer had some of those outfits as they had been burnt along with the rest of her possessions in the fire.

What a total waste, she thought.

Now that she had very few possessions she felt that she needed little else, she was content with what she had.

It was an eye-opener to realise that she did not need a lot of possessions to feel that she had enough and she was thankful that the fire allowed her to view her life in a completely different perspective and she liked what she saw.

Perhaps in the future, if she ever did find a new home

she would have fewer possessions and even fewer furniture, she decided, just the basics to keep a household running.

As she continued walking she noticed that most of the shops on this street were fashion retailers advertising their wares through the shop windows with the intention of trying to entice buyers in and she was glad that she was no longer gullible to those tactics and could so easily walk past them, without a second glance.

Chapter 16

She could not recall how she got here.

One minute she was walking past the retail outlets ignoring all the fancy clothes modelled by the mannequins in the window displays and the next she was about to turn the corner and cross the traffic lights when she was stopped in her tracks.

She was attracted by a light in this shop window and as she looked inside she could see some quaint antique items displayed on the shop floor. Her curiosity piqued, she paused for a moment, contemplating whether to go in or not. There was nothing to entice anyone in as the window display was rather non-descript compared to everything she had passed so far but for some unfathomable reason she found herself being drawn into the shop. As she pushed open the door a bell above the door rang out as though to announce her entrance and rung again as the door gently closed behind her. As she made her way to the counter her eyes darted around noticing the contents in the shop. Everything seemed eerily familiar and yet she was sure that she had never been inside this shop or even noticed it whenever she had gone for a walk during her lunch hour whilst she was working in this area.

As she approached the counter she saw an elderly gentleman standing there, peering at her through his circular rimmed glasses and she thought that he was smiling at her but she could not be sure. He reminded her of the character "Dumbledore" in the Harry Potter movies and if you added the moustache and long beard with the wizards pointed hat it would be difficult to tell the two apart she thought. His face was kind as he greeted her and asked her how he could help.

Bethany could not think of anything to say because his voice sounded identical to her grandfather`s and for a moment she was propelled back into time, when she was a very young girl, about four or five. She had fallen down and hurt herself and her grandfather had lifted her into his huge arms and dried the tears from her eyes and comforted her with such soft soothing tones that she had forgotten her pain and just fallen asleep in his arms. She was unsure how long it had been but when she awoke she was still cradled in those soft gentle arms and the feel of him close to her made her want to stay there forever.

He had always been so patient with her whenever he was looking after her, even when she screamed and shouted whenever she was hungry, flailing her arms in all directions looking for attention. She knew that he would give her a sweet then, but only if she became quieter and then he would put his hands in his pockets and slowly draw out different coloured ones each time, then unwrap the paper as she watched excitedly. Before he had placed one in her open mouth, it had already started watering as soon as she had seen the sweet. He would place her on his knees and move his hands up and down her back softly massaging her, so that she felt calm and relaxed with him. This was a routine for them both and she always looked forward to visiting her grandparents.

She was woken out of her daydreaming as the gentleman came around the counter, looking concerned for her as she had not uttered a word since entering.

She excused herself for being so rude and explained that his voice had reminded her of her grandfather who had passed away some time ago. He seemed to understand her as he nodded,

At the same time, he took her hand in his, patting it gently at the same time, more to comfort her than anything else. She was moved by this gesture of kindness from a total stranger and suddenly without any warning, tears started streaming down her face.

She could not be sure if it was the sound of his soothing voice or the fact that he had taken her hand in hers but it had been a very long time since she had been offered any comfort and all her defences evaporated as she stood there sobbing uncontrollably.

He guided her into his office at the back of the shop and left her alone for a while but when he returned he had a steaming hot cup of tea in his hands with a chocolate éclair that he placed beside her, urging her to have one. It reminded her of the sweets that her grandfather would offer up and just as she thought she could cry no more another bout of tears began welling up and started pouring out once again, as though a dam had burst open. As if from nowhere a box of tissues materialised and she reached out for one and wiped her tears and blew her nose. In between her sobs she tried to apologise to him but no words would come.

What a sorry sight she must have looked sitting in front of this stranger bawling her eyes out she thought but for the first time, after a very long time she felt safe and comforted.

The cup of tea was refreshing after her long walk and

she realised it was almost mid-afternoon and she had
eaten nothing since breakfast. Her stomach had started
rumbling after seeing the cake placed in front of her and
he offered her a sandwich as well which she didn't
refuse. They both ate silently together and after wiping
her mouth with a serviette he had placed with the
sandwich, without her noticing, she felt more like her old
self.

She was about to stand up and take her leave but
something deep inside her wanted to stay and speak to
him so she started with some small talk but he was asking
her so many questions about herself and he seemed
genuinely interested in what she was saying.

Although he was a complete stranger he was the first
 person to show a genuine interest in her welfare and
before she could stop herself, the words began tumbling
out of her mouth as she started to confide in him – all the
events from the moment she had met the stranger, to
being interrogated by the police, losing her credit cards
and job and then the house fire, nothing was left unsaid.

He listened with patience hardly interrupting her,
sipping the cup of tea intermittently but otherwise his full
attention on what she was saying. In between her pauses
he would offer words of comfort and this was sufficient
encouragement for her to blurt out all that had passed.

By the time she finished she had stopped crying and she
could not believe that she had spoken in this manner to a
complete stranger whom she had just met but there was
something about him that made you want to unburden
yourself. She thought of getting up and leaving to stop
herself from embarrassing herself even further but her

legs were just stuck to the ground and her body would not listen to her brain to move.

She thought that he was being kind to her by remaining silent and assumed that he was thinking of a way to get rid of her but that was the furthest thing from the truth. He had obviously been mulling over something very carefully.

After a short pause he suggested a temporary solution that would favour them both.

He explained that his wife was currently unwell and that he was about to close the shop, in order to visit her in hospital but at that moment Bethany had walked in, opportunely.

To him she had appeared out of nowhere, looking like an angel in disguise and he asked her if she would look after the shop whilst he went to visit his ailing wife in hospital. It was a short walk away and he would be back in time before closing.

He just wanted her to look after the shop for the short period that he was absent.

Bethany was uncertain as to how to decline his request without sounding rude. He had been so kind to her and she wanted to return the favour but she felt she was totally out of her depth. She had never enjoyed the pushy sales assistants in the retail stores at the best of times and she had no experience of dealing face to face with customers. Hers had been an administrative role initially then she had moved from one role to another then finally to project management, mostly dealing with management issues and deadline concerns, ensuring people were at the right place at the right time. She had never had any affinity with marketing or sales and she was content with leaving those tasks with others who had the knack for it. Now as she looked around the shop she felt at a loss as to how she could be of any help. However, as she took a closer look and made a mental note of all the contents in the shop she surprised herself as she started to recognise the value of some of the expensive pieces and could easily discern the lesser expensive items that were displayed in the shop.

Her father had been an antiques dealer and she would sometimes accompany him to the auction houses so she had some idea of what was in front of her, she now realised.

She did not want to be unkind and refuse him and she wanted to find a way to repay him for the generosity he had shown her but she felt that she was currently in no state to be taking on that responsibility and said as much.

He was not expecting that response and was hoping to change her mind and went on to explain that in the last month he had had no visitors into the shop and expected to see none so close to closing time so she would not really have to do a lot.

She did not have the heart to say no after that, especially as he had been so kind to her and so agreed with his request. It took only a few minutes to show her how everything worked and before she realised it, he had vanished and left her all alone and in sole charge.

Not knowing what to do next she sauntered around the shop inspecting the different items at close range, feeling some of them in her hand and debating their worth. There was a laptop at the counter and so she searched the internet to confirm her pricing and she was startled to see how accurate she was.

She realised that accompanying her father around the auction houses and the antiques shops had given her some good knowledge that had been buried somewhere deep within but had just needed a little bit of prompting to come to the surface.

As she looked around her there were books, bronze statues, tables, chairs, all in all, an assortment of antiques that would not go amiss in an auction she thought.

Just as she was getting engrossed in her little project of guessing the price of the items in the shop the bell above the entrance door rang, alerting her to a visitor and a man dressed in a tweed suit and hat walked in asking to see a specific piece. He was probably not much older than the elderly gentleman but he walked with a slight gait and held a walking stick with a lions profile at the face of the handle. Although he walked with an air of authority, it felt more as if he had an inferiority complex about him in the way that he conversed with her. Converse was probably too kind a word, it was more like a servant and master attitude as though ordering her to bring the item to her because it was beneath him to bring it himself, instead pointing in the direction he had seen it. She immediately took an intense dislike to him. Setting aside her personal feelings towards him she attempted to accede to his requests addressing his questions with a politeness she did not really feel, as she wanted to do her best for the owner of this shop.

After some dithering about, he came to the real reason for his visit. He asked her if they possessed a particular item in the shop and she had just moments ago seen it and so she directed him to it. After inspecting it closely he offered a price for it that he was willing to pay, stating that he would go no higher. Having just gone through some of the inventory in the shop Bethany knew that it was worth much more than what he was offering and debated whether to accept it or refuse.

The shop owner had clearly stated that he had had no sales this month but she was unwilling to let the item go for such a paltry sum when she knew it was worth much more.

She realised that he must have a very low opinion of her and he must think that she would not be aware of the true value of the item as he had treated her like a "common sales girl".

Bethany was not going to be treated with such disregard and decided to stand firm on the price and call his bluff. She explained, a might haughtily, to match his attitude, that if it came at auction the price offered would be substantially more than what he was offering and that she was aware of another buyer's interest in that piece.

It was obvious that he had set his mind on it and he could see that she was not going to shift her position. He also recognised that "this shop girl" knew what she was talking about, despite appearing to be a novice at this, so finally offered the price she had stated. Bethany wrapped the item carefully and handed it to him. As she placed it in his palm, he appeared to snatch it from her grasp but she was too ecstatic to care.

In a matter of minutes she had made her first sale and she felt like a true professional even though she had been quaking with dread inside and never faced a customer in her life.

Two more customers followed and again she was able to easily recognise the value of the pieces they had been interested in and get the sale value that the items deserved.

Perhaps selling was not as bad as she had feared, after all she thought.

She was sure that the owner had said that he had not made any sales for a month and that there had been no customers in the shop during that period yet here she was, already having sold three items so far. Perhaps she had misheard what he had said, she thought and she would ask him when he returned.

After that a few more customers followed, buying some smaller items that were not so valuable but with each sale, no matter how small, her confidence increased and her fear began diminishing.

She was unaware how the time had simply flown by as she had been enjoying this experience in a way that she never thought she would and before she knew it, the bell above the door rang again and this time the elderly owner walked through the door.

He locked the door and turned the sign around to show that they were now closed for business and he started to bring down the automated shutters at the front of the shop, flicking a switch that was conspicuously located at the side of the entrance door.

She had not noticed it before but it was an ideal precaution to protect the shop from intruders, given the valuable contents it contained.

She admitted to herself that her initial reaction, when seeing the shop for the first time, was one of incredulousness and disbelief that the shop could exist in the heart of a buzzing city centre because of its location, right in the heart of a city, where the pace of life was so hectic and frenetic.

When she had been drawn in, the ambience of tranquillity and serenity inside the shop were in sharp contrast with the feverish activity outside.

The elderly gentleman asked Bethany how she had managed as he made his way into the back office. Bethany explained that she had had a few customers and had sold some items. She had taken cash for all the items she had sold and she had deposited it in a cupboard in the back office as she felt vulnerable with wads of cash stuffed in the till. She had handed out invoices with the sales, just as he had instructed her to do, should she sell any item. She added that the cash would tally with the receipts.

He was surprised to see how much she had sold and said as much, appreciating the fact that she had made light of her inexperience in sales, after all.

She explained that she had surprised herself and that it had taken no effort on her part to be make those sales as the customers had just rolled into the shop. All she had to do was to point them in the right direction, as they had come in with the express intention of purchasing something specific in any case. All she had done was to just guide them in that process and complete the transactions. It was quite a simple role that she had played she added.

As she had fulfilled the favour he had asked of her, and certain that there was no more to detain her, she walked in the direction of the cloakroom to take her coat. Wordlessly, she put on her coat and started making her way towards the exit, mumbling her goodbyes and feeling somewhat disheartened as she did not want to leave the old gentleman.

For some reason she had felt a deep connection with him and she simply could not understand how it was possible to feel like this for a total stranger but she no longer wanted to outstay her welcome.

He must have been contemplating something, perhaps he wanted to pay her a percentage of the sales she had made, she thought, just like salespeople earning commission on top of their salaries.

She would refuse him because he had given her something that had been missing from her life for a very long time, a sense of fulfilment and a small measure of purpose.

His attention seemed to be miles away as she approached the exit from the back door, ready to walk out but he called after her and it was then that she realised that he had been trying to find the right words before he spoke to her.

He asked her if she would be willing to listen to an offer that would be of benefit to them both.

She had shared earlier that she had no place to live and at this moment he wanted a reliable person to look after his shop whilst he took some time to help his wife with her recuperation at home as she was going to be discharged from hospital in the next few days. He asked her if she would be willing to look after the running of the shop as she had clearly showed the aptitude and he was certain she was more than capable of managing it on her own.

In exchange he would offer her accommodation, free of charge, as a temporary arrangement, whilst she found a place to stay.

He continued to explain to her that his house was large enough to accommodate a number of guests and she would have the freedom to do as she wished, without being indebted to them.

He added that she was welcome to stay with him and his wife for as long as was necessary, until she got back on her feet and furthermore, the house was well furnished so there was no need for her to splash out on any unnecessary expenditure.

At least Bethany would be unencumbered, financially, she thought so she listened attentively to what he had to say before making such a life-changing decision that would entail her making a commitment that she had not made provision for. She had got used to being totally independent and it had suited her well until now but it seemed that fate had other ideas in store for her, ever since her encounter with the stranger.

It seemed to her that she was the one that was most benefitting from this arrangement and she had no intention of taking advantage of his generosity. She explained how guilty she felt if she accepted his offer but he waived her doubts aside and insisted that it was the other way around, that his wife and he were the real benefactors of this situation. She realised that as she had no job offers in the pipeline, nor found a suitable place to stay she would seriously consider it.

He proposed that she accompany him to see the house at that very moment and she wondered if he feared that if she had more time to consider his offer she would reject it outright.

Before she had time to respond, she found herself sitting in his car, making their way to her new accommodation.

She was unprepared for how fast her fortunes were suddenly changing but decided that she would make the most of her opportunities. In the past she had veered on the side of caution, only to realise afterwards that she had made the wrong decision, something that she understood with the benefit of hindsight.

They had closed the shop, making sure it was secure before heading out of the crowded city.

She recognised part of the route they were taking and she started to feel anxious when it became evident that they would be passing her burnt down house. She gripped the side of the passenger seat so tightly that her knuckles began turning white. She did not realise it but her teeth were clenched and her jaw started to hurt as her gritted teeth tightened even more. The car turned onto a side road that she had never taken and she suddenly breathed out a huge sigh of relief as the car was steered towards another direction, away from where she thought they were heading. He had taken a short cut and after leaving the heavy congestion they came onto some scenic routes where the traffic was very light. Large oak trees lined the street and most of the buildings in this area had basements with gated entrances that prevented pedestrians from falling into or trespassing into them. She was surprised by the lightness of the traffic, as she was familiar with part of the route they had taken, and she had always encountered a queue full of cars on that stretch of the road. It seemed to her that the cars were moving aside as soon as they saw them approaching just to let them through, just as they did whenever the Emergency Services approached, but of course this was only her imagination she said to herself as they made their way further along the road.

Chapter 17

In no time at all they arrived at their destination. The car crunched onto the crescent shaped gravel drive as it was steered towards the house. Either side of them were well-manicured lawns with an imposing but beautiful magnolia tree at the centre of the lawn. The fragrant pink and white star-shaped flowers were in full bloom and their scent filled her nostrils as she alighted from the car. Her eyes were drawn to the building in front of her because it reminded her of her own house, the one that had burned down, only this house was larger in dimension but the roof was the same shape and the positioning of the windows were just as she remembered her own house to be.

The similarities were a little disconcerting and she did not want to be reminded of them.

She stepped out of the car and the crunching sound as her feet touched the winding gravel stone path to the house were the only sounds in the silence and seclusion of this place. She noticed the distant sounds of birds chirping sweetly to one another, as if welcoming a new guest and as she walked in to the house that feeling of welcome reverberated through every nerve and cell in her body, despite not a single word having been uttered. The house itself had a homely feel to it and the house maid who stood there to allow both her and the old man in had extended that welcome with a wide, genuine smile which appeared on her face the moment Bethany entered. The maid then opened her arms out wide to give Bethany an embrace, as though she was a long lost relative who had finally found her way home. As Bethany stepped into the threshold and into the maids embrace it was as though all her worries just melted away. Bethany remained in that embrace for longer than she deemed appropriate and thought that perhaps the maid must have instinctively realised that Bethany had needed to be in that comfort and warmth of it so she remained in her arms for a little longer. Bethany could not understand how a complete stranger was displaying such affection towards her. In the weeks and months that followed, she herself learnt how to open her own heart that for now, was so broken and shattered that it refused to allow anyone in. She had never experienced such a welcome before and it took her by surprise as she walked into the hallway.

The maid and the old man must have had some telepathic communication going on between them because whilst he remained at a distance, the maid showed Bethany around the large house, almost like an estate agent, showing a prospective buyer around, only in this case, the maid did not have to highlight any of the advantages of the place.

The old gentleman remained downstairs as he wanted Bethany to make up her own mind about staying, without applying any undue influence upon her and Bethany, in turn, realised that he was allowing her the freedom to do just that, by remaining downstairs.

He had been hoping to see some signs of approval from her as she had entered the house but she had kept her feelings hidden as she did not want to disappoint him if she decided to refuse his offer to stay, because he had already been so generous to her.

As she was guided downstairs there were four rooms that branched off from the hallway.

There was a formal dining area showing off views of the front manicured lawn and the magnolia tree, that she had seen earlier taking centre stage. In this room was a suitably positioned window seat from where to sit and admire that landscape. At one side of the room, standing against the wall was an antique cabinet, made of walnut and a matching etagere, placed unobtrusively in the corner beside it. At the opposite end of the walnut cabinet stood a large comfy sofa. Bethany could just see herself sitting on that after enjoying a substantial home cooked meal and, once again, it reminded her of her home, which had a similar layout, save for its smaller dimensions, where she would do just that after devouring her supper and feeling completely satiated.

In the middle was an oval shaped dining table that could easily seat sixteen diners. All of the furniture was well-matched in this room, with the maroon velvety coloured cushioned chairs complimenting the light walnut colour of the furniture. The dining room was adjacent to the kitchen and as she turned into the hallway again, she Continued further along the corridor and was shown into the drawing room. As she walked in, her attention was drawn towards an ornate fireplace against the middle of the wall, bordered by small white columns above which stood delicate ceramic figurines supported by a rectangular shaped base. Pastel peach coloured sofas, made of a velvety material were spread out in this room and complemented the light blue coloured walls, once again leaving the impression of carefully selected colouring to match throughout this area too. As she walked further inside the room she was surprised to see one wall covered with wallpaper of a design she had never seen before and it too blended so beautifully with the whole of the room that the vision it created was quite spectacular. It was as though someone had taken a photograph, enlarged it and then placed it onto this wall. Its magnificence was such an eye-catching spectacle that it took Bethany`s breath away as she stood there, open-mouthed, startled by its presence in this room and awed by the beauty it exuded.

It felt to her that it was created just so that it could be placed right here, in this room.

It was a scene of flocks and flocks of life-size pink flamingos stretching out on the lake as far as the eye could see. They were standing slightly lopsidedly, with one foot in the air and one planted firmly on the bed of the lake and they were staring back at her. For a moment Bethany was taken back to the time when she had visited Kenya in late November one year and witnessed them in their feeding ground, on the shores of Lake Nakuru. She remembered the tourist guide telling her that these flamingos were born with grey feathers, which gradually turned pink because of their diet of shrimp and blue-green algae which contain a natural pink dye, called canthaxanthin. They would stand with one foot in the air, almost as if they were going to hop on one foot but deciding against it, at the last minute and getting caught between poses in mid-air. The guide had said that they adapted that stance and would alternately keep the other foot in the water in order to keep their bodies cool in the hot and suffocating heat.

She felt overwhelmed with emotion just standing and staring back at these beautiful creatures. They were one of her favourite animals, along with dolphins and elephants because they each carried themselves with such grace and elegance. On that visit to Kenya she had also been able to witness elephants at the water hole washing themselves and cooling down by blowing gallons of water through their trunks and onto their backs, the water streaming like a jet wash, down their backs, as they hosed themselves down.

Forced to take her eyes away from this scene, she turned to look outside the large oval shaped window which gave views of the even larger rear garden and she could not wait to explore its every nook and cranny but the maid interrupted her and led her out of this room and into another one. It was obvious that this next room was designed for relaxation because to one side were large-sized cushions resting against the wall. They could easily be repositioned onto the floor, inviting anyone to stretch out and lay down to have a relaxing snooze. To the other side were several sofas, some reclining and some three or four seater versions. Once again the presence of order and tidiness made this room so bright and airy and as a shaft of sunlight wound its way through the room, like a focussed laser beam, she could feel its warmth encompassing her like a blanket. She could easily picture herself laying down on one of the sofas, on a beautiful sunny Sunday afternoon, temporarily closing herself off from the outside world, just as she used to do, in her own home. She quickly put those thoughts to one side to bring her back to the present.

This room led into a good sized conservatory and this, in turn, opened into the garden patio, which she cursorily got to glance at.

As she was led back to the hallway she noticed how each of these rooms downstairs contained very little clutter but the layout of every piece of furniture, sofa, painting, or ornament, was positioned to take maximum advantage of the space in each of the individual rooms and it gave the appearance of spaciousness and comfort at the same time. She was surprised not to see the rooms cluttered with antiques as she had seen in many house owners who were Professional antique dealers, including her father.

When she was younger and did not understand his love of antiques or their value, she had often wanted to put them all up for sale because of the dust that quickly gathered around them and the time and amount of effort it took for her to clean all the rooms that housed them. She recalled having to be meticulous and careful at the same time to handle some of the items delicately, fearful of damaging them if she was careless. Thankfully all the pieces were left intact when she had finished.

As she was led into the kitchen it too reflected the order that she had seen in the other rooms. There were no items on the work surfaces and she was surprised to see it was bedecked with all the latest conveniences when she was allowed to inspect inside the drawers. Kettles, toasters and mixers that one normally saw laid out for all to see on the work tops were hidden away, each, had their own place inside. Like all the other rooms, the kitchen was also a good size and could easily cater for a small party of twenty or so people. It was unlike her kitchen which could only cater for a maximum of four people in it before it felt overcrowded, she thought. The kitchen also overlooked an expansive garden which was separated by large bi-fold glass sliding doors and it was a seamless transition to step straight into the garden from here as it was on one level making the indoors and outdoors merge so naturally well together, in keeping with the current trends in house design.

She was surprised not to see any wall-mounted television screens in any of these rooms as the sound effect of a cinema surround would not have gone amiss in these large uncluttered rooms.

It was so lovely to see how the elderly couple had made this into a warm and inviting home and she was certain that this impression of casual, uncomplicated elegance would also be repeated upstairs.

Once again, she was directed back towards the hallway where she now found herself in front of a huge winding staircase that was also ornately but simply decorated.

As the maid guided her up the stairs, she could imagine herself being happy, living here and she had the feeling that whilst she was living here she would be cut off from the rest of the world, protected and cocooned by these loving people.

This time the maid left her to explore each of the individual rooms upstairs whilst she made her way back down so that Bethany could go round on her own to decide which room she wanted to occupy. As she made her way around, she noted how each room had its own uniqueness about it, in some the furniture was as though it had come from the antique shop it was so elegant and strong, once again, every piece matching and belonging in the room. Even the bed covers and pillows and cushions all had matching sets so that the whole room would not have looked out of place in a costume drama television series. However, in some rooms, there was sparse furniture, just a bed lamp on top of the bedside cabinet and a four piece chest of drawers with a landscaped picture resting above it, but they all shared one common feature, and that was the stunning view of the different aspects, of the garden.

She was given the choice to decide which bedroom to make her own and as she went through each room she was unsure which one would suit her best as they all had their own distinctive character that set them apart from each other.

Finally as she was giving up hope and contemplating on mentally drawing straws, to decide which one to use, she entered the last room and immediately knew this was it. She had inadvertently walked past this room when she had first come upstairs but now as she stepped inside she noticed how the sun`s rays were filtering into it as shafts of light flickered on the carpet silently dancing and welcoming her in. She had not seen anything like this before and she felt as though this magnificent show had been waiting for just the right person and the right moment to reveal itself and she just happened to be in the right place to witness it. As she moved further inside her attention was drawn towards the window seat through which the sun`s rays were more focussed giving it the appearance of an angelic aura covering the seating area. It was as though she was being offered a cloak of protection and as she walked towards the window, all she had to do was to surrender to it. As she sat on the window seat she felt a huge arm gently caressing her spine working its way up from behind the top of her head moving to the base of her neck and slowly yet softly making its way down to the base of her back and she drew out a long sigh of relief without really knowing why, yet at the same time, feeling safe and warm and comforted. She was unsure as to how long she had sat there for and as she turned her head to look at the garden her eyes were drawn to an even more magnificent view outside. This room overlooked the large rear garden, which had a patio and chairs at the front, and then steps leading down to a large green lawn with an array of the most beautiful flowers that had been strategically placed to create a distinct border between the patio and the lawn. The window in this room overlooked the centre of this huge garden which gave her an uninterrupted view of the whole landscape in front of her, however, it was not this that drew her gaze outside.

It was the sight that was obviously the centrepiece of the whole garden. From where she was she could clearly see three large bronze "child Buddha`s" placed on a square plinth in a row, side by side and surrounded by a waterfall that cascaded gently down onto a circular platform that wound its way slowly down to the ground.

From her room it was difficult to see where the ground finished and where the circular platform started because they blended in so well, the only telling sign was that one part was drowned in water and the other part totally dry. She could not fathom what materials were used but she suspected that it may have been some form of toughened glass because it was glistening in the sun and the water as it hit this circular feature appeared to sparkle and glisten like silver.

She could not wait to inspect this feature more closely but at the same time she did not want to move from her position because she wanted to drink in the feeling of calmness and serenity in the room.

So she sat by the window for a few more moments to take in the feel of the sun on her back as it warmed and caressed her whole body, re-enforcing the feeling of warmth and security even more as she sat there and pondered on the events of the last few days.

Her fortunes were beginning to change and she wondered what was on the horizon.

Chapter 18

She was unsure how long she had been sitting by this window as she awoke from her reverie and she realised it would have been very rude to stay up there any longer so she made her way back downstairs.

The maid must have been patiently waiting for her at the foot of the steps and as she came to the bottom of the stairs, she was lead towards the rear garden.

She walked on to a large patio that led down to three wide steps onto the large expanse of lawn. There were large earthenware pots placed either side of the steps, containing effusive bunches of various flowers whose bright and pastel colours seemed to invite you to step onto the beautifully manicured lawn that stretched out as far as the eye could see.

First it was the rooms upstairs, then downstairs and now the hidden gems in this garden, everywhere her gaze fell and every direction she looked, something caught her eye.

As she viewed the landscape in front of her, little could she have guessed when she first set eyes on the house that it was hiding all these secrets. As she slowly explored each nook and cranny of this large garden it began to unravel its secrets to her.

Just like the front garden the grass here, in the rear garden looked so well maintained and everything appeared to be in its exact place, there was no clutter of overgrown plants or vegetation and the lawn was so well looked after she felt fearful of stepping on to it and making imprints and spoiling the effect.

She hadn`t noticed this from the view upstairs but as she walked into the garden she noticed a large imposing oak tree to one side of the house around which a bench in an almost pentagon shape had been fashioned around. It was the ideal place to allow one to sit in the shade of the tree and as she looked closer she noticed that the bench was part of the tree in the way that it was made of the same material because it was difficult to distinguish how one was separate from the other. The bench must have been designed to look identical to the sturdy wide oak tree and its trunk formed a support to use as a rest for one's tired legs after walking around these extensive grounds. Everything about the garden, the lawn, the tree, the border fencing, the flowers and even the water feature had been carefully selected to give it the appearance of calm and tranquillity.

The further she stepped onto the lawn, the more her feet sunk into the grass and it was as though she was walking on a velvet carpet, the grass cushioning her feet and supporting her at the same time. She had never walked on grass like this before, it was almost like walking on air and it felt so light and soft under her feet.

She couldn`t wait to see the waterfall that she had seen earlier, from the upstairs bedroom and as she moved even closer, she was not disappointed. The water was enclosed inside natural rocks that had been positioned in such a way as to allow it to cascade down two levels onto what appeared to be the ground. "This ground" was made of toughened glass and as the water ran underneath her feet it gave the impression that she was walking on water.

The cycle completed as it ran back to the top level,

cascading back down again. She could see why it had been positioned here because the gentle flowing of the water could be heard from the conservatory that was nearby.

She could imagine sitting in the conservatory and allowing the sounds of the gentle cascading water lulling her into sleep.

As she looked around she noticed that at the other side of the waterfall was the outline of three separate Buddha statuettes. They were all in different poses, perched on a stone-like plinth whose dark greyish colour matched the rocks in the waterfall. The way this had all been designed was as though it was all formed from the same rock because there were no gaps between the plinths or the statuettes. All the Buddha statuettes followed the same flowing movement and she wondered how long it must have taken to plan and then implement. Some stonemason must have really crafted his skill to perfection in order to make this impact and it made her wonder if the ideas originated from another plane, because their effect was so unusual and delicate, and yet strong and powerful.

As she approached them to take a closer look she noticed something strange. No matter what angle she approached them from, they all appeared be staring back at her, like the painting of a person's face whose eyes felt as though they were always on you.

She wondered if it was some form of trickery of these three-dimensional forms as she could not imagine how this could be possible so she made a mental note to ask the owner when she returned to the house.

For the moment, though the sound of the waterfall as it flowed into the ground, sent her into a calm and reflective trance as she stood and just watched, absorbing the sounds of the birds chirping in the distance and the rustling of the leaves on the trees, stirred by the gentle breeze which cooled her whole body.

In her trance state she noticed that there were some words transcribed onto each of the Buddha statues just below where they posed so she moved even closer to read the inscriptions.

There were different messages under each one.

As she looked at the first Buddha she noticed that his face seemed to be laughing.

She had heard somewhere that the laughing Buddha brought wealth and prosperity to the household in which it was placed but she could not recall where she had seen this. As she peered close to read the inscription the words seemed to be talking directly to her and stated "Tomorrow is the most important thing in life, comes into us at midnight, very clean."

She moved on to the next Buddha and the inscription below that one read "It is perfect when it arrives and puts itself in our hands" and the next inscription on the third Buddha read "It hopes we have learned something from yesterday."

The message the words were imparting all went above her head as she had been so preoccupied with finding a resolution for the current state of affairs that had befallen her but she made another mental note to ask the old man all about it.

For the moment she decided to just live in the present

moment as that was all her brain could cope with. She let her gaze follow the outline of the house and then back to this beautiful garden and marvelled at how they both complemented each other.

She felt deep inside that she was in the right place for whatever was to come and a deep knowingness in that instant intuitively told her that she was going to be happy here.

All she had to do now was to agree to the proposal that the old gentleman had offered her and to move in with her sparse belongings.

She could imagine being loved and cared for here, just as she had been, when her parents were alive, even though she had only been here for a very short time.

The welcome she had received from the maid and the temporary arrangement she was being offered here would allow her to re-gather her perspective so that she could decide on what course of action to follow next.

These surroundings were far better than she could ever have asked for and an opportunity like this may never come her way again, she concluded.

She realised that people went all over the world and paid a lot of money to visit and stay in ashrams and sanctuaries to cut themselves off from the world in order to find inner peace and a sense of purpose to their lives. Yet here she was, being offered the opportunity to do just that, in this beautiful setting, without having to visit any of those far flung places or even pay for the astronomical fees that some of those places charged. When taking all of this into consideration, she thought that she really had nothing to lose.

So she walked back into the house and decided to accept the old gentleman`s offer.

Chapter 19

After collecting her belongings from the Bed and Breakfast she settled into a routine, as the days passed into weeks and the weeks into months.

Her hope of ever finding the individuals who had intentionally burnt her home down had evaporated and worse still the insurance company had categorically refused her claim, informing her that arson was one of the categories that was not covered under her home insurance.

She had even surprised herself by the effortless transition, from being unemployed, without an income or idea as to what step to take next, to working in this antiques shop and finally coming full circle. She regretted not pursuing her dreams more forcefully earlier on in her life and rued how she had wasted so much time. Now, finally she had started to live from her heart. It had taken her experiencing all these calamities in her life, from the loss of her parents, then later her job, then her family home, to realise that this was what she should have always been aiming for. At the time it felt as though everything was working against her. Everything had been snatched from her one moment and in the next moment she was fortunate to have re-discovered her first love once again and now here she was, having come full circle.

She had finally found her passion, working in this Antiques' shop and although having never had any experience in sales or retail, everything the old gentleman had showed her came easily and naturally to her.

She put it down to the fact that antiques had been in her blood for so many generations, from her great grand-father who had bought his first collectible car set and then her grand-father who had showed her his railway model collection which had been handed down to her father. Her father, for as long as she could remember, had also caught the bug and spent his whole life in the antiques business, beginning as an apprentice with his father, where he swept the floor and made the tea in his antiques shop. As he watched his father, he gradually accumulated a good eye for antiques and his early finds included Glass, Chinese and English Porcelain and Paintings. He travelled around all the auction houses, sometimes being away from home for days, becoming an expert in his field and at the same time, collecting his own antiques and making a very good living from it, by selling some pieces whenever the demand was there. Her father loved history and in particular, the stories behind how the antiques were acquired. Eventually, it was this passion that led him to specialise in miniatures and he became a world authority on those creations between the 16th and 18th century to such an extent that his judgement was highly valued by his peers. Even the jeweller, Martin Norton, who was known as the doyen of dealers, trusted her father, once to attend an auction on his behalf, as he himself was incapacitated at the time. He had every confidence that her father would only buy the best pieces, even if the prices were a little too high and he was not disappointed.

Her father was also on the vetting committee for jewels and portrait miniatures for the Grosvenor House Fair, the

European Fine Art Fair and the British Antique Dealers' Association.

His shop attracted passers-by with a treasure trove of exquisite objets d'art and he even had many international clients who became firm friends because of his kind and gentlemanly manner.

Her father seemed to have a good eye as to what would be in demand and what would not sell well and without realising it she had inherited that from him and whenever the opportunity arose, she loved to accompany him on his adventures. She had lost count of all the innumerable journeys, up and down the country she had accompanied him on and although she could not recall them very clearly, the one thing she did remember was how excited she was each time she went with him. Even as a young girl, the smells that each of the auction houses evoked, always made her feel fortunate that she was a part of this world.

For her it was a natural part of the world and she felt that she was blessed to gain an insight into how people lived in years passed. It always fascinated her, even to this day, what different items people kept in order to hand down to their offspring. They always took great pride in keeping these things in pristine condition and in some cases they were locked away in a special cabinet or storage box, stored away in a little forgotten corner of the house never again to see the light of day until one day, quite by accident, some of them were discovered and identified as lost treasures. Even if some of them may have had no intrinsic value the way they had been lovingly cherished gave her great pleasure and the memories that were often associated with them, with the stories behind their acquisition never failed to surprise and excite her at the same time.

When she was a teenager she was sure that her father was grooming her to step into his shoes and she very much wanted to comply with his wishes, not so much to please him but because she was genuinely interested in all things antique. The more and more he explained to her about the origins of certain objects the more fascinated she became and she went to great lengths to investigate and research the history of some of the items that she had the great fortune to hold in her hands.

It was one of the reasons she had decided to major in History of Art at University, allowing her to understand both ancient, modern society and culture so that she could gain a better perspective when looking at the antiques.

However, her parents' death and the subsequent upheaval that followed had put paid to all those dreams. She had been forced to find a job and as one year followed another she became so absorbed in her work that nothing else mattered. She became totally consumed with making her way up the corporate ladder that she had forgotten all about those dreams until now.

So as she worked diligently in the shop she found that all the information she had accumulated over the years that had been stored in the back of her mind was now resurfacing as and when the appropriate time came, all whilst she was being shown the ropes. It felt like the old man had replaced her dad and he was now acting as her mentor, reminding her of her one true passion and life now looked so different.

Even her own outlook had taken a complete transformation that she no longer recognised herself from the person who had once worked tirelessly and with just a single focus.

After several attempts to submit evidence to prove that her house had been set on fire, intentionally targeted by person's unknown, she had come to the conclusion that the authorities had colluded in her downfall but they had not counted on her tenacity. She thought that she would chose to fight them another time, and on her own terms, but for the moment she would bide her time, laying low and continue to gather conclusive and irrefutable proof that she could then present and confront them with.

It was unfortunate that they had threatened a lonely old lady with the same fate as her, so that she had no choice but to withdraw her statement and fail to corroborate Bethany's accusations of a cover-up.

Finally Bethany had concluded that no-one would benefit from pursuing her case regarding the torching of her house any further. Other than giving her the satisfaction that she, a minnow, had won her battle against Goliath, there was no sense in chasing rainbows and so with reluctance, she had finally come to accept that it was best not to pursue the insurance company regarding the loss of her home.

She mentioned this transformative effect to her mentor and he explained it to her in the following way:

When uncomfortable things rear their heads, we are really being asked to question the path we are taking and to change course. Events or circumstances show us things one step at a time but if we don't take notice we are forced to take notice and this begins, at first, with a gentle nudge but if we ignore it then there is a gentle dig and if we choose to ignore that, then finally we are completely knocked off course. When this happens, it forces us to take notice and to make changes in our life because it becomes obvious that what we are currently doing is not bringing us any joy or fulfillment and if we continue on our present trajectory and continue ignoring these events, we will never find any happiness and our lives will continue to remain empty and meaningless.

We can compare it to a dirty cup of water which has to be emptied before it can become clean. Do we want to continue drinking from that dirty cup and continue taking in all the pollutants or do we want a fresh cup to refresh and invigorate us.

In the same way, when you look back at your life, you may question why you lost your job, your home, in fact everything that you held dear. You will have come to realise that if you had continued to head in the direction that you were going in, you would never have found any happiness but instead, just continued to remain mired in sorrow. In your case, someone or something forced you to change direction and now, with hindsight, you can understand how much better your life has improved.

You see we misunderstand these situations and we think that the Universe and everyone in it is against us and it is doing its best to make us struggle and feel helpless but the Universe is on your side and what it is doing is informing you that what you are doing so far does not serve your higher purpose.

Our emotions are the litmus test and we have to be prepared to pause and make an accurate assessment without letting our emotions carry us away. Whenever we make rash decisions, in the heat of the moment, we realize only afterwards, that we have made the wrong decisions and so it is so important to take a step back and view it all as an observer.

You see, we know this to be true because when our emotions are impacted so profoundly and in such a forceful way, our whole world feels as though it has been turned upside down and that is the sign that we need to pay attention to, because that gives us the opportunity to review where our life is headed and to change course.

Many people will face different situations based on their own circumstances, some will feel the loss of a partner through a messy divorce or falling out and always blame the other person. It is very easy to pass on the responsibility and blame anyone but ourselves but we must find the courage to assess what part we had in that separation so that we can then "repair" ourselves and be ready to embrace new and more meaningful relationships.

It can apply to any situation, not just relationships, it can be health issues or financial struggles, but whatever it is that we feel we are lacking or missing we have to embrace the challenge and not hide away from it.

He went on to reinforce it by recommending a daily habit that he often implemented to remind himself of this:

If we check our emotional status on a daily basis and measure whether we are joyous or sad, angry or calm, frustrated or fulfilled, then we are able to be better informed, with where we are going wrong. We can decipher what makes us unhappy, what we don't want and determine more clearly what makes us content and what we do want. If we use this as a compass and are more discriminate in choosing what we really desire from our heart's perspective then we will become better tuned in to that which continues to make us happy so that we can focus on those things more regularly. When we focus our mind and thoughts in that direction then our internal vibrations will conversely begin to attract and match our external environment and we will begin to live in alignment with our soul. This will increase our ability to be surrounded by those things which warm our hearts and as we practice this on a more regular basis we will raise our vibrations so that we will be able to detach ourselves from the feelings of pain hurt and struggle. This is not to say that we will live in a state of constant happiness and be ignorant of the struggles of those around us but rather their state of unhappiness will not be the reason to bring us down.

Unfortunately we live in a culture of blame and become blinded by false promises because that is what we are used to and what we are constantly surrounded by.

It is only when we move away from that and take a moment to look more deeply and introspectively at our own selves that we will see the wood from the trees and so be able to move forward and embrace all that life has to offer.

She felt that this was a very deep and important message for her and she pondered on what he had to say and if she were honest with herself this circumspection bought her to the same conclusion and she agreed with what he had shared because it was what she had experienced in her own life up until now.

The old man began to share his wisdom with her at odd moments in the shop and she felt as though she was his pupil and he, the teacher, had appeared now that she was ready and open to learning.

Days passed into weeks and weeks into months and sometimes the old man would accompany her to the antiques shop now that his wife had fully recovered.

Initially, when Bethany had agreed to work in the Antiques shop, he could see how everything came naturally to her and so he had left her on her own while he stayed with his wife at home to help her recuperate. His wife had undergone a knee operation but there had been complications, which had resulted in her stay at the hospital. When she had been discharged from the hospital he had employed a carer to help manage her day to day needs and this also helped her to become confident around the house once again. On days when the weather permitted, he often accompanied her in the large garden during her walks to help in her recuperation. Although his wife had always been independent, the operation had left her vulnerable and he realised it would take some time for her to return to "her old self". The carer was very patient and compassionate and as each day came and went he could see that his wife was slowly improving and he wanted to offer his support and encouragement by being there for her.

Bethany had shown she was very capable of running the shop in his absence and he had wanted to be with his wife, whilst she was recuperating.

The couple now had the opportunity to spend hours together, chatting, walking or just sitting in silence, in the garden or in the lounge. These were the moments he treasured with her, especially when they were in the garden, discussing re-arranging the positioning of the bedding plants or buying new plants or flowers for the garden and. That was her passion and he could see the joy reigniting her, once again, whenever they talked about it.

After a month, as her health begun to improve, she became more active, wanting to take up her hobbies again and experimenting with cooking or pottering around in the garden. He realised that now she was back to doing the things she loved, her joyful and bubbly character had re-emerged and he would often find her humming tunes or singing to herself but when he interrupted her, she would stop. He could see that he was in her way now that she had recovered and so with mutual consent, he returned to the things he loved doing, meeting people and working in the shop.

For Bethany, time seemed to pass quickly as she settled into a routine and she was surprised that eight months had passed since her first encounter with the old man.

At quieter moments in the shop, she would take the opportunity to go out for a walk allowing herself to be away from the routine. In reality, her life did not feel like routine any longer as each day was different to the next and she always looked forward to waking up to see what the new day would uncover. She realised that she would never fall back into the boring routine of her previous life of getting up, going to work, coming home, eating, going to bed and repeating the same thing over and over again.

Besides, she could no longer identify herself with that monotonous lifestyle and, for that, she had this old man to thank for.

How had her life changed so drastically and suddenly-both, from an emotional and a psychological perspective.

The trust that she had felt in humanity when she was a young girl had slowly dimmed until it had completely faded but now, it was slowly returning. Ever since meeting the elderly gentleman, her heart had naturally begun to open slowly and the experiences she was now having were much more heart felt and she felt that she was no longer living from her mind or letting her mind take control of her.

In the past, the sudden and unexpected death of her parents had resulted in her having to close off her dreams, as her survival instincts had kicked in and led her to take up a role in the financial world. Despite carving out a successful career with financial stability, she felt she had sold her soul and simultaneously closed off her heart. Since the death of her parents she had closed her heart to deny her true feelings or emotions from surfacing, fearful of exposing her vulnerabilities and she had carried on by immersing herself in her job at the expense of everything else. No doubt she had had some wonderful holidays which had appeased her inner demons temporarily but outside of work she really had no-one that she could call her true friends, no real social life and certainly no family to turn to

The fact that she was finally able to fulfil her dreams of

following in her father's footsteps and starting to live a life of passion was all the evidence she needed to show her how far she had come.

Now everything looked completely different and she felt that she had finally emerged from decades of darkness into the bright light like a butterfly shaking itself free from its protective cocoon.

Her life was now worthy of living because she was learning to live from her heart.

If she could summarise how her life had been up to now she could probably say that it was akin to an automaton, a soulless existence, living by the rule of her mind.

Now her trust and faith in humanity had been restored, simply by making one life-changing decision. That of helping a complete stranger in his hour of need. She herself had been in a precarious predicament but for a moment she had forgotten about her own situation and come to the rescue of a stranger. Now look at how everything had transpired, since making that fateful decision. She felt that the world was at her feet and she could finally achieve her full potential. It was like a caged animal being trapped one moment, and then the next, suddenly emerging from its imprisonment, to roam and wander freely.

She had been looking at the past and blaming other people for her own failures and shortcomings and letting them steal her future and her happiness but not anymore.

A new and unexpected world had begun to open up to her and she was going to grasp this opportunity with both hands and never let it go. A new page was going to be written from now on and she had the power to write her own script and she was determined that from this moment onwards she would not allow anyone to deter her.

She thought she had clearly mapped out her life and knew exactly where she was headed but here she was now in an entirely new direction not knowing where she was heading but intuitively sensing that she had finally found something to truly believe in, a worthwhile cause which involved helping this elderly couple to run their antiques business while they spent time with each other. Time to allow his wife to recuperate from her illness and for the old gentleman to stop worrying about the running of the shop, while he was with his wife.

He had seen how competent she was and her knowledge of antiques gave him the assurance that she would be perfect to take responsibility of the shop in his absence.

Bethany realised that she had never really been satisfied with her life and yet she had never questioned it, until now.

It was only after she had been fired and found herself in a precarious position that these questions had begun to be thrust into the fore-front of her mind. Although she did not have all the answers yet she felt confident that her present predicament, if you could call it that, was the opportune moment to re-assess her life in finer detail.

When she compared herself to this couple she realised that what she was missing was someone to share all her troubles with, some-one who could help her and guide her and comfort her and support her through all the hardships that she had yet to endure.

She had noticed their family portraits in the rooms

downstairs and if they were anything to go by, she could easily see how much they complemented each other and how much, after all these years (she was unsure how many) they obviously loved and cared for each other. The elderly gentleman always spoke fondly of his wife and despite each of their idiosyncrasies they were always willing to meet each other half way. The gentle way that they spoke to each other with their loving gestures had been an eye-opener for her. To witness how relationships could be forged in this way, with empathy and patience further rekindled her faith in humanity.

It reminded her of the kindness of her neighbour and she made a mental note to speak to the old man about taking a day off to visit her and thank her for the temporary shelter and kindness she had given to Bethany at her hour of need.

Chapter 20

As luck would have it, one day, he suggested that she take some time off, as she had been totally committed to helping him in the shop and had not had the opportunity to take some time out for herself in the several months she had been there.

At first she was surprised by this request as he was aware of her pleasure and joy at working at the shop. For her, working there was akin to being on holiday, as there were no deadlines or targets to meet and she was continuously learning new things every day.

She felt under no pressure at all and the experience of working in the shop was like nothing she had ever experienced in her working life. In fact she wondered how it could even be called work, when in reality, each day was a joy to be alive as she was passing her time doing the things she loved.

Nonetheless, she agreed with his request and decided, on the spot, to take the opportunity to visit her previous neighbour. She had plenty of time to spare and initially began wondering around, window shopping. The clothes that were being modelled by the mannequins in the shop windows, no longer had the appeal they once did and as she loitered inside the shops, casually walking around, browsing and running her fingers through the different clothing material, to sense how it felt, she realised that it was a recurring habit she had indulged in, in the past, each time she contemplated buying any new clothes. Some habits were so deeply entrenched that they would not easily leave her and this was one of them. She accepted that and without wasting any more of her time, as she had no intention of buying anything, she walked out and found her way to a florists and then the local confectioners to buy some flowers and a box of chocolates for her neighbour and made her way there.

As she entered the station, she realised that on one of the last occasions she had used the Underground, she had been fired from her job and then robbed on her way home. That memory seemed to be so far in the distance now that she was uncertain, for just a brief moment that it had actually transpired. On this journey, however, she had nothing to fear, as it passed uneventfully and before she knew it, she was standing in front of her neighbour's door, poised to ring the doorbell.

She had not called in advance, to notify her of her visit, partly to surprise her but also knowing that she would be at home at this time of the day, as was her customary habit. Her neighbour was very surprised to see her and at first failed to recognise her, especially so, as Bethany looked so different. She looked radiant and happy and the bags under her eyes that had once been so evident, when she was living with her, had vanished and even her hair appeared more fuller and thicker, if that was really possible. Her drooping shoulders had become a thing of the past, as she stood there in front of her, tall and erect carrying herself with an air of authority that had not been there before. As her neighbour peered closer, she noticed how the whites of Bethany's eyes appeared even whiter and the pupils so healthy and alluring, that for a moment she wondered if it was indeed Bethany standing in front of her.

Realising she had dawdled a little longer than necessary at the door, she welcomed Bethany in and led her into the living room.

As they sat and chatted Bethany explained how her luck had changed since meeting the old man and how she was now working at the Antiques shop. Her neighbour remembered how Bethany had always wanted to follow in her father`s footsteps in the Antiques business and understood now why Bethany looked so different. She thanked Bethany for the flowers and chocolates and they sat chatting, whilst eating the home-baked marble cake that she had made the day before, accompanied with some hot brewed tea.

Bethany told her about her circumstances, leaving out the finer detail as they continued laughing and sharing happier memories of the past, when Bethany`s parents had been alive and were living next door. Those memories no longer felt like a deep wound had been afflicted upon her and Bethany was surprised by her own detached reaction.

She would share this experience with the old man but in her heart she realised that the past no longer affected her as it once had.

Time just flew by as they sat and chatted and before she realised it, it was time for her to return to the shop before it closed and Bethany stood to take her leave. She promised she would keep in touch and not leave it so long before she came back to see her again.

Her neighbour was glad to know that Bethany was safe and well and after the customary farewells, Bethany took her leave.

In her happy mood she had forgotten about the destroyed house and the possessions she had lost and as she left the neighbour`s house and gazed in that direction no feelings surfaced. It was all a void, as though nothing had ever happened.

In that moment Bethany realised how far she had come. Clothes no longer attracted her and she realised that being attached to material things, as she had been in the past, was fruitless as she would never take her possessions with her, when she died. She liked to dress smartly but she no longer bought things, just for the sake of it. In fact, she could not recall going shopping for clothes since her predicament and she smiled at the realisation. It felt as though a weight had been lifted from her shoulders as she made her way back to the shop. As she walked, she felt her feet were not even touching the ground, as though she was walking on air and she could not wait to share this experience with the old man.

Chapter 21

The journey from the neighbour's house to the shop was uneventful and, if anything, went by in a haze.

She was approaching the shop and just as she turned the corner, ahead of her, coming out of the Antiques shop, her shop, were the two men who had been responsible for turning her whole life upside down. These were the very same men who had set fire to her house, causing her to become homeless and losing her job.

Immediately all her emotions became muddled up and from the calm blissful disposition a moment ago, instead, she now felt a burning rage begin to consume her. The two men were to blame for all of this and she decided that she would confront them and demand an explanation as to why they had singled her out for such callous treatment.

Just as she was about to rush from the corner of the building from where she was emerging, she immediately stopped in her tracks and realised the uselessness of these reactions. As she hid behind the façade of the corner shop window and watched furtively they walked in the opposite direction towards the parked car they had left by the shop and made their way inside it.

As they drove away she watched the car disappear, until it was no more than a tiny speck of sand, uncertain if she should move from her spot, afraid that they may return.

She stood there for what seemed like hours but was probably just a few minutes, until she was sure that they would not reappear and allowed her rapidly beating heart to return to its normal beat.

She was not sure whether to return to the Antiques shop as she was sure that the men must have spread a web of lies to the owner and she anticipated that she would, in all likelihood, now lose this job too.

She had been completely honest with the owner, from the outset. She had disclosed every detail of what had happened and left nothing out as she wanted to start all over again. It was better, from her perspective, to start a new chapter in her life with a clean slate.

She thought she had left her past behind but now all her uncertainties returned and wondered what lies the men had spun.

In the past it had not been difficult to persuade her ex-employers to let her go and she was certain that the old gentleman would also be easily deceived by their dishonesty and now would want nothing to do with her.

On the other hand he may take her side and keep her on, despite what they may have said.

She was in two minds now, indecisive and questioning herself. It was a situation she had not experienced for so long, after being in the company of the confident assured old gentleman and the feeling left her with a fear in the pit of her stomach. A fear that felt alien to her.

All her hard work and effort was now in tatters, she thought, and she would never be able to find a job like this.

The last few months had whizzed by so fast but at the same time, she had experienced so much joy and security that she did not think she would ever find that inner contentment ever again.

She was just about beginning to understand herself so

much better after all the guidance and counselling he shared with her every day but now all that would come to an end. It was like a butterfly emerging from its cocoon but being forced to emerge too early and having its wings clipped.

She looked forward to the adventures of a new day whenever she awoke but now even that was being snatched away from her.

She would have to start all over again.

She decided it was better to face the wrath of the owner and have it all over and done with instead of speculating as to whether she would be out on the streets or not.

So with a heavy heart she trudged slowly towards the shop and opened the door with a false smile on her face, pretending to be unaware of the strangers' presence earlier on.

He smiled back at her when she entered and asked her if her expedition had been fruitful and she nodded, mumbling to him at the same time, about her visit to her neighbour's.

As he looked at her, he could see that she was visibly upset, despite her smiling façade and suspected that she may have witnessed the presence of the two men in the shop. He took her to the back store room, sat her down and explained what had occurred moments earlier.

The two men had come barging into the shop demanding to know of her whereabouts but he acted confused and incoherent, unable to understand who they were referring to. His manner led them to conclude that he was just a tired old man, who knew nothing about her.

Realising that the information that they had gathered

(about her employment there) must have been incorrect as they had seen no visible trace of her presence there, they looked around the shop and quickly made their excuses and left.

Any doubts she had about her future quickly evaporated.

He then continued to explain to her that he had asked her to leave the shop as he had suspected that they would be calling.

She was fascinated by how he had known this and even more mystified as to how the two men had learnt about her presence in the shop but she would ask him about this on another occasion because for the present, she was just relieved that her job was intact and that she had a roof over her head.

A few more weeks passed and her sense of security had returned although she was watchful of the people who visited the shop and more alert whenever she went outdoors, to ensure she was not being watched or followed. She even took precautions by taking different routes to and from the shop in order to confuse anyone who may be watching or following but nothing aroused her suspicions.

Her mind was still preoccupied by how the old man had suspected the arrival of the two men and she was going to ask him directly but events, once again, proceeded to divert her.

After another busy day at the antiques shop she was returning home with the old man accompanying her in the car. It had become a ritual now, that he would drive on the way to the Antique's shop and it would be her turn to drive on the way back. Bethany could still not understand how the traffic opened up to pave a free path, whenever he drove, but the roads always seemed to close up and become busy, whenever she drove.

It was on one of these occasions when she was driving back home with him when an incident shocked her to her core. They were approaching a busy main road when to the left of her vision and out of the corner of her eye, she saw a car suddenly pull out onto her path. The movement was so fast and so sudden, that she was sure that the driver had become impatient to be quickly on his way that he had mistimed it, probably thinking he could squeeze his car through the small gap that had appeared. As a result, that car was almost upon her and she could do nothing but brace herself for the inevitable impact to her left side.

The oncoming car was so close that she could even see the drivers look of terror on his face as he realised his mistake and prepared himself too for the obvious collision. The movement caught Bethany so unexpectedly that she had no time to react, brake or even slow down and as she loosened her grip on the steering wheel getting ready to protect her face, somehow her car swerved into the empty oncoming lane, which moments earlier was full of cars lining up behind each other, bumper to bumper in the busy rush hour. It was as though a hand had forged a clear path in the opposite direction and her car was steered effortlessly into the opposing lane. The inevitable crash of metal on metal was suddenly and inexplicably averted and without knowing it her hands grabbed back their hold on the steering wheel once again as her car veered back into the correct lane and continued on its journey.

She was uncertain as to what had just occurred as she was sure that she had done nothing to avoid the accident but something had certainly taken over and guided her car to safety.

Several emotions began coursing through her body and she had to supress the urge to stop the car in the middle of the road and, instead continued driving, as though nothing had happened.

She drove in silence to their destination, like an automaton without feeling, and as they arrived at the circular driveway that was covered in pebble-stones it alerted the occupants of the house of their arrival. The crunch of the tyres on the pebble-stones awoke her from her robotic state and for a moment she could not recall how she had managed to drive safely all the way home.

She felt numb at the moment and the old man must have been aware of her state as he gently coaxed her into the house and urged her to come into the conservatory to calm her nerves and allow her emotions to fully express what they had not been able to, earlier on.

She sat for a while, dumbfounded and in shock, beside the open doors.

The view of the greenery in the garden and the birds chirping in the summer air, began to bring her mind at ease, and slowly, she begun to come back to her full senses.

The warmth of the sun in the conservatory began coursing through her whole body and the cold numbness she had experienced earlier on slowly bought her back to full awareness of where she was and what had occurred.

A cup of tea had been placed in her hand and she sipped from it, glad to have the opportunity to pause for a moment and mentally understand what had just taken place.

However, no matter how hard she tried, her brain was so confused by what had occurred, that she could not see through the fog that she was mired in.

The old man gave her time to finish her tea and as she placed the cup beside the table next to her he spoke gently but purposefully as he could see the confusion in her face.

He began by telling her that they had both averted a serious accident and that a Greater Force had intervened on their behalf. It was obviously not their time to die yet and so their Guides had jumped into action to ensure their survival. They rarely interfered with life and death situations but there was obviously something that the Universe had in store for them and so it was necessary that they took the action that they had.

She listened intently without saying a word but nodded her head to indicate that she had understood what he was saying.

Since her own personal calamities, and, at the gentle prompting of the old man, she had started to read books on philosophy and spirituality, in order to awaken her own understanding of other worldly matters and so what he had shared with her had come as no surprise to her.

She realised that her past experiences all added up to the wake-up call that had prompted her to take her life in a different trajectory. Otherwise, she would be like countless millions of people who had been raised to believe what others had told them, in effect, following a script that we are told to follow, from the moment we are born, to the time of our death.

The old man himself admitted, that once upon a time, when he was at a low point in his life, he had turned to the same things as she had, in order to find some meaning in his life. Instead of blaming others for his predicament, he had taken responsibility to turn his life around and started his own journey by reading a variety of spiritual books by different authors, such as "The Celestine Prophecies" by James Redfield and "The Alchemist" by Paulo Coelho and so many more. He still had those books in his library collection and she was welcome to read them whenever she wished.

Bethany had done so and discovered that they had opened her to an awareness that she had completely forgotten about.

When she was much younger, she was always in nature, spending days in the garden or by the beach or in the woods, whenever the opportunity arose and for her, it was her second home.

She had always felt easy and comforted when in that environment.

She recalled now, how the birds would come and sit by her, unafraid of her presence, twittering away, as though having a conversation with her. Even the dogs and cats were drawn to her but as soon as she was joined by another human being, the birds would fly away. She had always been aware, even then, of her affinity with God's creatures.

She even remembered going to bed at night or walking

in nature and seeing beings that were both so vivid and yet unusual, that she was sure if she stretched her hand out, she would be able to touch them but she was always too fearful of them, because of their unfamiliarity and chose instead, to hide under the covers of her bed at home, or run away, if she was outdoors, sprinting so fast, that she was sure they would never catch her. At that moment, she did not have the courage to hang around and find out what they wanted from her.

In any case, her mum had warned her never to speak to strangers and to shout or scream, to attract other people's attention if they ever came near her. Although this was not the same as the "real people" she encountered, she did not want to take any risks and always chose to keep her distance from them. They seemed to appear and then disappear at random and she could never understand how it was possible, to vanish so fast. It was like being hidden inside a dense fog, with just you and them, then suddenly emerging out of the thickness as the fog evaporated and it always happened so fast that she didn't even have time to blink. She never felt afraid of these visitations as she felt they were always magical and mysterious and she was certain that they really existed but she did not know how to approach them or how to communicate with them.

As an only child, whenever she was in her own company, she would often talk to herself and even ask questions, sometimes out aloud. Often, she would hear the answers, inside her head, wondering where those answers came from her. Now, after reading all these books, she had become more aware that those answers had originated from her "Guides" and sometimes her

"Higher Self" or Angels, opening her to a world that was both unique and indescribable.

She had turned to her mother for an explanation but her mother always dismissed her and scolded her for making it all up and gave her pictures of different Gods, Goddesses and even images of Christ or Buddha to place under her bed or place in her pocket so that she would be distracted and protected by them simultaneously. Bethany did as she was told but never thought that she needed any protection from them as she, unknowingly, felt safe in their presence. If she was in bed, and she felt fearful, she would curl up and hold on tightly to the doll she kept by her pillow, so no-one could separate them. It often worked because she felt comforted by her presence and would instantly fall asleep, not realising it, until the following morning.

At school, she never mentioned these experiences to anyone else as she did not want to be called names or excluded, for having imaginary friends and so and as time went on and she grew older, she began denying their existence, thinking she was being foolish. Eventually, her denial of their existence caused them to gradually fade away, as they stopped appearing altogether.

It was accelerated even more, after her parents' death, when she felt it was time to leave all that behind. It was useless holding on to those fairy tales and she made a conscious choice to recognise that it was finally time to grow up and become a responsible adult and live in the real world. She had to begin looking after herself now that she was all alone and so she made a conscious decision to force herself to abandon it all. She had even relinquished all her dreams, but now, after reading these books, she had begun to rekindle those long lost memories and begin to live out her dreams.

Chapter 22

She started to rediscover the skills she had left behind as a child.

The old man had told her to begin to meditate every day, as he had done, in order for her to rekindle those skills and develop them even further.

She had asked him how he had begun his exploration and he shared with her, how he had been introduced to meditation and from there, advanced his skills by attending various classes and reading books that helped him to continue his education in this field. Instead of telling her directly what steps she should take, he had given her examples of how he had applied the teachings and built them naturally into the rhythm of his own life, even suggesting, that she peruse the library of books that he had accumulated over the years, to introduce her to these concepts. Those books contained topics and teachings from various luminaries who were at the top of their field and she could choose whichever ones appealed to her most. As Bethany browsed through the books on the shelves in her spare time, she saw a variety of material and admitted to herself that she had never heard of any of the authors, names like Diana Cooper, Eckhart Tolle, Deborah King, Denise Linn, Dr Wayne Dyer, Dr Bruce Lipton and countless other luminaries who were at the top of their field.

On other occasions, she noticed how he kept himself informed of current trends in this area by attending on-line classes to connect and share ideas with other like-minded individuals.

She had even overheard him conversing with someone on the internet, during one of these sessions and she had been so intrigued by the discussion they were having, that she patiently bided her time to speak to him about it afterwards. However, the session seemed to be interminable and so she decided to just dawdle in the background, hoping to catch a sentence here or there, to understand what was being said but it all went over her head. They had been talking about how to "tune in" to "Guides" and the "Higher Self" and other practical techniques to instil in their daily lives. One of the speakers, whom she overheard, called Marilyn Alauria, was explaining how everyone has access to other realms but only, if they are willing to be open to them. She had gone on to expand that once upon a time, it was believed that only people who had special abilities had access to these gifts but it had now become obvious, that no special skills were required and that these abilities were accessible to anyone who was willing to take the time to learn about them. She had overheard her telling her audience, how these techniques allowed the merging of the emotions of the heart with those of the mind, so that instead of constantly being in conflict with each other, they are continuously working together. By being consciously aware of this, each person was empowering themselves to take control of their own lives, instead of allowing life to control them, she had added.

At one point during the session, Bethany was so mesmerised by what she was hearing, that it was as though time had stood still. Nothing seemed to matter anymore and for a moment she was carried into a world that seemed to be suspended, free of time and space. She was unsure how long she had remained in that state but what she was certain of, was that it was because of the meditation they had been performing at the close of the session, that she had overheard. It had left such a profound and deep imprint upon her that she could not wait to experience it herself but before she could begin, she wanted the old man to give her some further insights as to why it left that impression upon her. She would try to make sense of everything she had heard, no matter how long it took and she planned to integrate it all into her life, gradually but surely, just as he had.

Since this "new life" she had begun to become a lot more inquisitive about everything, often questioning herself and sometimes, the old man, if she could not fully fathom what she was hearing. So after he had finished, she had asked him to enlighten her further.

As usual he did not wish to force his own beliefs upon her but referenced their sources, to give her the opportunity to carry out her own research and instil them into her own life, as she wished. He was content to point her in the right direction and let her make up her own mind about what resonated with her and to experiment with what worked for her and to discard what did not.

He had explained to her, that everyone has unique ways of learning new skills and it was one of the reasons he did not wish to force his own ways of learning on her. In addition, educational institutions and the larger communities do not recognise the concepts that he was presenting to her and so are unable to cater for those who want to learn about these things. He hoped that perhaps, at some time in the future, these teachings would be accepted as a part of life but until then, people would struggle to come to terms with the merging of the heart and the mind, until they could find ways to address the missing piece of that jigsaw.

She understood what he was saying and was grateful that she had been given an opportunity, at a very young age, to access a small part of this and experience it, although it had been curtailed by the untimely demise of her parents.

She, in turn, was very impressed that a man of his age was still so engaged with his continual development, especially the ease with which he worked his way around technology, something that she had still not quite fully grasped yet but now she had more time, she would take the opportunity to become more proficient. The moment that thought crossed her mind, she realised that her old patterns of thinking were coming to the surface again. The old man had told her so many times, that if she really wanted to begin living from her inner heart, then one of the most important things that she should learn, was to stop judging people. Unless she was in their shoes, she could never know what situations or circumstances they had faced in their past so if she kept an open heart, remained non-judgemental and was more compassionate towards them, she would progress immeasurably. She had to constantly keep reminding herself of this, in addition to the other useful tips that he had shared, as it was the only way she could realign her own life.

He had done the same when she had appeared in his shop for the first time, patiently listening to her inner turmoil and offering help at the opportune moment.

Bethany was re-patterning her life from the inside out, just as the old man had been doing, for so long now but it was a slow and gradual process. She could see that it required continuous attention and that it was a life-long quest that would never stop.

He had told her, almost from the first time that they had met, that if she wanted to lead a meaningful life, it was not about being judged by one's wealth, popularity, Education, or by trying to be perfect. It was about doing the very best in all our endeavours and continuously enriching our lives with knowledge.

There was obviously more to it than that, but for the moment it was a good place to start, he had said.

She had woken up to begin transforming her old patterns and stories and the beliefs that had come with it.

The meditation practice that she had started helped her with all this too and she noticed how calm she had become, feeling less anxious and stressed.

He had explained to her, how Eastern philosophies had embraced Meditation, centuries ago and understood its benefits but the West had dismissed the practices until the last fifty or so decades. After many studies, even science had discovered that people who meditated regularly kept certain ailments like cancer, heart disease and diabetes at bay, together with other life-changing benefits. In particular, research published in a Canadian scientific journal, showed how the DNA structure in our genes was being impacted, physically lengthening the protective caps on the end of chromosomes (known as telomeres.) As yet the full impact of this research was still being assessed but since reading about this, he had changed his lifestyle and it was one of the reasons why he was always so full of energy.

He went on to explain that ever since he had started meditating many, many years ago, he slept better than he had ever slept before and he felt younger and less stressful. Furthermore he was able to change his whole life so that he was now much happier and fulfilled in ways that Bethany could never imagine. He himself had never imagined that he would be able to turn his life around because he was constantly running around chasing happiness, thinking he would find pleasure in external things, in the hope of finding joy and contentment but instead, all he found was distress and anxiety. When he discovered the benefits of meditation, he could sit in his own place of silence and patience and whatever problems he had, solutions came to him, flowing effortlessly and without struggle.

He told her that he would tell her more later, when there was more time but Bethany had the feeling that he was drip-feeding her information, a little at a time, in case it became too overwhelming for her but she did not mind. She had gone through a lot this year already and perhaps she was not quite ready to hear it all at once.

She had an inkling of the results because she could see he was always relaxed and happy and had the appearance of always being joyful. Even the interactions with people he met were always so positive, that she rarely witnessed him losing his temper. In fact, now that she thought about it, the whole time she had been in his company, she could not recall a single moment when he had raised his voice.

Bethany was already aware of the other benefits of meditation but she had never paid much attention to it all until now.

So every day Bethany would wake up a little early to begin her own practice.

At first she found it was very difficult to focus as any minor noise or interruption would unsettle her and jolt her "awake" causing her she to become increasingly frustrated that she could not come to grips with it. Usually, learning new skills excited her and she was able to integrate them into her life seamlessly but this was the exception.

So she asked the old man why it was so difficult for her and he explained to her that initially when we introduce new concepts into our lives, our mind puts up a resistance because it is in the habit of old patterns which are not easy to discard. To compound it, our mind is constantly on alert, looking out for any threats, as it wants to keep us in a safe and comfortable environment and sees these new approaches as a threat. As it assess these threats, there is a constant chatter in the mind, which is further fuelled by our fears and our desires. When we meditate, we are trying to silence those thoughts and thus, it creates a resistance. Another factor, he had continued to explain, is that as we grow older, the thoughts that have shaped us, our experiences and the influence of our culture, whose thoughts and values drive and influence us, also play a role in adding to the mix of chatter going on in our head and this flow of movement that is "running counter to the crowd" adds more fuel to that resistance.

So it is only through constant practice of meditation, do

these processes slow down so that we become more proficient and over time, it becomes easier. He compared it to riding a bicycle for the first time. Initially it is difficult to manoeuvre around and balance yourself but with time and practice, it gets easier until you can ride it without anyone by your side waiting to catch you, if you fall.

Bethany decided that despite the resistance, she would continue her resolve to be able to meditate knowing that eventually it would become a natural process.

He had explained that she did not need to sit in one place. She could be out in Nature, walking, cooking or cleaning, or whatever took her fancy at that moment. This helped her greatly and improved her practice even more.

She still continued observing the old man for any further insights.

One day, during a quiet lull, she took the opportunity to ask him about the incident weeks before in the shop, concerning the unannounced visit of the two men.

So he shared a valuable and in depth response. He told her that for centuries now, we have been living in such a way that we have allowed our minds to have total control over us. This is understandable because during that time, we were living in an era where our basic survival mattered. We needed to find shelter (housing) to keep us safe and secure and we had to work, in order to earn money to feed and clothe ourselves and our families. That was our daily struggle for several centuries because we had not become economically sufficient to sustain ourselves in the long term but after decades of economic development, it no longer became an issue for many countries.

The other aspect as to how we have allowed the mind to take control is to protect ourselves from painful experiences. Although it is a natural reaction to want to protect ourselves from them, we begin forming habits that cut us off from our hearts and to avoid feeling those traumatic emotions. By cutting off our hearts we have become less compassionate, less forgiving and essentially less human so now, more than at any other time in our existence, we need heart empowerment, where we begin living from the heart and make decisions guided by our heart rather than our minds.

He has found techniques to balance the communication between the heart and the mind and one way that he has learnt to live from the heart is, by being open to the messages that his inner guidance gives him. He starts his day by speaking to his "Guides," as though they are present beside him and having a conversation with them every morning. He greets them and thanks them every day for standing beside him and for supporting him. He then asks them to guide him in the right direction during the day and help him at the same time, so that he can talk to whoever he needs to talk to, see whatever he needs to see, hear what he needs to hear, go where he needs to go, and smile at whomever he needs to smile at. He has complete faith in this process but he is not complacent and does not hold on to any expectations but remains confident, that whatever outcomes arise, they will all serve him well. The main point is that he does not just listen to the responses he receives, but he immediately acts on them and it is this regular practice that has kept him safe and, in turn, helped the people around him. Using this technique, he is giving room for both the mind and the heart to work in conjunction, in harmony, rather than in conflict. He is living consciously, each day, paying attention to the signals and responses he receives and honouring them by taking action. By living in this way, he also understands that what he wants, also wants him and is looking for him and attracting him because that is the energy he is sending out. Others who are "listening" to that frequency become attracted to it and that cycle is consistently repeated, as long as he continuously engages in this way.

That is one of the greatest secrets that anyone can follow, if they are able to grasp the concept, he had told her.

Bethany was even more curious with this explanation, as she has never heard of it being spoken in this way but in the back of her mind, she knows the truth of what he has said, as her past experiences as a young child point to the existence of these Guides, Angels and Spirits.

Now everything makes complete sense and she is keen to learn more.

If she had not been witness to the earlier events with the two men arriving unexpectedly at the shop and with the turn of events that she herself had been experiencing, ever since she had met the old man, she would have labelled him "a crazy old man".

She had been in his company for long enough to realise that he possessed an intimate knowledge of the connection between himself and other dimensions that gave him access to things she could not quite fathom.

The way that he always seemed to attract the right people at the right time and even the manner in which customers were being drawn to the shop. It had all seemed very odd and until now, she could not comprehend how it was happening.

Before she had been dismissed, she had often walked in the direction of this shop, during her lunch break, just to browse through the shop windows but she had never noticed this place. It was so inconspicuous, tucked away at the very end of a parade of other more vibrant and more appealing shops that she had never given it any attention, often walking right past it.

As far as she could tell he never advertised, either in the papers or on any of the social media platforms and there were no fancy colourful signs in the front shop window, to entice customers inside. Yet despite all that, customers were drawn in.

So all this provided her with sufficient evidence to prove that there was something in what he was saying and even her own "accidental" meeting with him, so many months ago was a case in point and they could not all be just coincidences, she thought. Besides, she could not come up with any other explanation and so she accepted everything he shared with her, with an open mind.

Chapter 23

As the days pass into months Bethany settles back into her routine and the episode of the two men has long been forgotten.

She takes great care to observe the old man even more closely and begins to notice things that she had never noticed before.

On the days that the old man is at the shop the whole day, Bethany observes how he takes regular breaks throughout the day and she realises that these breaks occur every hour and he carries out different activities, each time, taking a few minutes.

One day she sees him washing his face with warm or cool water, running his fingers through his hair at then massaging his head. The next time she notices that he is smiling to himself and looks as though he has gone into a trance. On yet another occasion, he whispers a word repetitively to himself and no matter how many attempts she makes to come close to him, to hear what he is saying, she fails.

Finally, one day, she plucks up the courage to ask him about it.

*He explains to her that he is giving his brain small rewards throughout the day, to keep his mind active so that he does not become bored and there is even less likelihood of him feeling or becoming stressed. As well as meditation, these minor rewards during the day bring him so much pleasure that he is able to accomplish a lot more, than if he did not practise them and he is able to appreciate and value his life so much more. He goes on to explain to her that he has been doing it for so long now, that these routines have become so ingrained that they are a natural process of his life.

She can observe the truth in what he is saying because he is always so vibrant and full of energy and she wants to experience this too.

She could recall a time in her life, when she was working full-time and putting so much energy into her work that by the time she finished and arrived home, she just about had sufficient energy to prepare and cook a meal for herself, before flopping in front of the television watching useless programmes, that required little or no mental pressure on the mind. Sometimes, she was so exhausted that she would wake up the next morning, to find dried food leftovers on the plate in front of her, evidence, if any was needed, that she had fallen asleep on the sofa, without even undressing or moving upstairs, to bed.

So she asked him to explain to her, precisely what it was that he is doing, so that she can start to feel lively and alert, just like him.

He explains to her, that every hour he does one minute meditations but he does not sit quietly in a room cross-legged as some "gurus" would want you to believe. Instead, he is actively continuing his work but conscious, at every moment, of his thoughts and subsequent actions. As he takes this approach, he is not carrying out his tasks like an automaton, without any thought, but he is fully aware of what is happening all around him, with his senses alive and alert to share in that experience. At moments when he is quiet, he recalls beautiful experiences that he has shared with his wife, such as sitting in the garden, taking in the sun and having a picnic, whilst the birds are chirping away in the background. He evokes all his senses to maximise his experience, feeling the sun on his back, smelling the freshly-mown grass, feeling the back of the sun-lounger supporting him, the taste of the freshly-pressed lemons in his lemonade drink and it gives him so much pleasure that he forgets any anxieties or worries that he has and instead, comes up with solutions that he is currently facing. Other times, he is grateful that he has a wife who is so kind, loving and caring and he reflects on all the wonderful memories they have been able to share together. Sometimes he may think about one word, for example, it was the word "happy" today. He was mulling it over and over in his mind to compare experiences in his life that would match this feeling. He has even gone so far as to keep a book, that lists all the joyous experiences he has shared and when he reads it daily, he is reminded of how fortunate he is. By living in gratitude like this, he derives so much pleasure and that pleasure increases with each day that passes. That is not to say that he always has a "Polyanna" outlook, but he is more optimistic about overcoming any challenges that he may have to face.

So as Bethany continues to observe him, she begins to follow his example. She is not always successful, but she no longer derides herself, for missing or forgetting the practices he has shared, but instead, talks to herself kindly and with sympathy. This is something that he had shared with her, so that instead of criticising herself every moment, she was learning instead, to speak to herself with love and kindness.

Once again he has shared more pearls of wisdom with her so that she can understand why this is so important.

He explained that when we are young we are constantly absorbing information like a sponge, right up until our teenage years, simply because our brains are wired to work in this way. Whatever we are taught in schools or society, or, whatever we witness at a young age, those things impress upon us so deeply that we then replicate those behaviors. Those behaviors, in turn, become our beliefs, whether they serve us or not because we believe there is no other way. For example, if you are constantly criticized, then your belief system may tell you that you are not good enough and so, as a result, you constantly learn to criticize yourself. This behavior continues until adulthood and we gradually build on those belief systems, further perpetuating those negative behaviors. Unless we learn that it no longer serves us and are willing to change those old habits and soul-destroying patterns, that pattern of pain and suffering becomes so embedded that we find it difficult to be removed from it.

Bethany realised that in the past she would speak to herself very critically, often chastising herself for minor misdemeanours. She realised that it only started after her parents' death and when she began working. She would often be corrected or criticised for minor indiscretions, at work and the more it was repeated, the more she began to believe the imperfections that were highlighted by others. This was when that critical self-talk within her began and it exposed all her "flaws". So instead of highlighting the gifts that she possessed she began to focus on her deficiencies so sharply, like a torchlight that it burnt deeply into her. With time, as it continued unabated, it eroded her confidence but she kept it in check to prevent her from becoming depressed. She had known of colleagues who could not deal with it and had taken time off from work to address these challenges and some had returned to work, with more compassion and empathy towards others feelings. However some had not and she had assumed it was because they had moved to other firms, little realising until now, that were unable to move out of that dark void that had probably taken hold of them and perhaps surrendered to it to give up entirely. She wished now, that she had done something to help them but she realised that at the time, she had not been armed with the knowledge she had now and so would have had no way of assisting them. Besides nobody would want to expose their own weaknesses by discussing their brittle mental health, and just like her, many carried on regardless, ignoring or not able to face their inner demons.

In order to help her build her confidence, the old man had asked her to begin by standing in front of a mirror and saying the words "I love you" at least three times a day. Bethany recalled that the first time she did this she felt really stupid and doubted that it would make any difference and wanted to give up there and then. However, so far the old man had not been wrong about anything and she had learnt to have faith in his teachings and so despite her initial reservations, her determination to transform her life the way that he had, spurred her on and she persisted with it every day.

As she did she felt her heart begin to open up little by little, like a flower unfolding its petals and bursting into its fullness, showing off its true beauty and unicity.

She was finally learning how to bring harmony back into her life and start to let her heart rule her, instead of her head. It was a concept that she had followed automatically when she was young and it always came to her easily. She realised that her closeness to nature had enhanced and helped her to do that and at that time she had never questioned or doubted that way of living. Abandoning and closing off her heart had cost her dearly but she was now in the right place to erase those old patterns and begin afresh.

Bethany often wondered how the old man, even at his age, continued to have such a zest for life.

He explained to her that it was because he always remained inquisitive and would question everything that he did not understand. He even shared a maxim with her to encourage her to follow him and that was that it was "never too old to learn".

He attributed this as one of the many reasons that he felt young at heart and intended to remain like that for as long as possible. He continued to explain to her that he viewed age as just physical development in human life and a number that should not limit us. In the same way, there should be no rules in place that tell us that once we get old, we should stop learning. Knowledge does not increase with age but if we want to improve our knowledge then we should be open to learning and that is one of the reasons why he still felt young and he would continue to be a prime example of these concepts.

With each day that passed, all that Bethany had experienced, before meeting the old man became a distant memory. All the pieces of her life were finally coming together like a jigsaw puzzle but there was still one final piece, yet to come, that would completely stun her.

It took her some time, to come to terms with the impact of what was revealed, and it coincided with the very first meeting she had, of the stranger she had rescued.

Chapter 24

As was their customary habit, every third Sunday, the old couple would invite a group of friends to a gathering which involved about fifty individuals.

Each person would come with hand prepared meals of a variety of offerings, always vegetarian, to share with everyone.

It was on one of these occasions that Bethany was encouraged to attend.

In the past she wanted the couple to have their own privacy and would make herself scarce by disappearing to her room, until every-one left.

However, it was a warm summer's day, too hot to spend in her room and so she decided to accept their invitation.

She had helped the housekeeper, to prepare a dish for all those attending and as the other meals arrived, she helped her to set out several tables at the back of the garden so that everyone could help themselves to the buffet selection.

It reminded her of the picnics that she had shared many times with her parents in the back garden or in gardens that belonged to the Natural Trust. Whenever her mother knew they were going out, she would prepare a simple but delicious meal for all of them to share, during those days out. They would be neatly packed into a picnic basket, with each person's special requirements catered for and it felt like a special treat for her whenever she unwrapped her food because it was done with such love, care and attention. They rarely ate in the coffee houses at the National Trust properties as it tended to be quite packed in there and expensive. They always preferred to be outdoors and wanted to make the best of the weather as they never knew when the sun would come back again.

There was always a routine they followed. Once they had entered the grounds, they would park the car in the allotted space provided and make their way to the buildings, walking around the perimeter to take a closer view of the architecture and then go inside to view the treasure displayed in these mansions. Some of the items in there, dated back hundreds of years and had been passed from generation to generation and so were unique and invaluable pieces. They were often kept inside a bullet proof glass display and Bethany always liked to guess their monetary value. She had acquired her father's knack of valuing the different pieces accurately and it was a game she shared with her father, to see who could guess their value to the nearest penny. Those early days were what had got her so interested in antiques, in the first place.

After finishing their tour of the interior, they would then walk to the picnic area which the owners had assigned especially for that purpose. Those summer days were the days she enjoyed the most because the whole family spent quality time together, relaxed and at peace in each other's company.

She was interrupted from her memories by the sound of distant laughter and conversation.

As she stood alone, she compared this garden to the

ones held in trust by the National Trust and noticed that it was not dissimilar to those properties she had seen because these gardens were also huge and well-manicured and contained many different flowers, some of whose names, she had never heard of, or encountered before.

She started to mingle with the people who had arrived as she did not want to feel the odd one out, introducing herself and sharing small talk with them.

Eventually, the old man came to seek her out and took her aside, as he wanted to introduce her to someone, who had once been staying in the house. This "guest" had been adopted by the couple and as he had grown older, he had helped with the daily maintenance of the garden as well as the house. He had left a few years ago but kept in touch with them, intermittently, and had returned today, unexpectedly.

Bethany had heard him being mentioned very rarely, by the old couple but now that he had returned, she was certain to hear more about him.

As the old man introduced them, his eyes lit up and she could see how proud the old man was of him, by the way in which he spoke to him and the manner of his respect towards him.

Bethany held out her hand to shake his, in greeting, and raised her gaze to meet his eyes.

She found herself standing in front of the stranger, whose life she had saved and for a moment, she stood motionless, unable to say anything.

She could not understand how their paths had crossed again or even how he had survived the fatal injury that had been inflicted upon him.

There was so much she wanted to ask him but other people interrupted her to greet him and she impatiently stood to one side, to allow them to talk to him, waiting for an opportune moment, to gain his full attention.

He was conscious of her moving aside and took her hand in his and let her stand beside him, whilst the others carried on talking to him. They all seemed to know him, and she observed how easy he was with everyone, and how he made each one of them feel important, in their own way. It was a trait, that reminded her of her father because he had a similar knack of putting people at their ease, even when they were in unfamiliar surroundings and as she watched him, she noticed how he shared a lot of his other mannerisms. The way he lightly touched his forehead, to brush aside the lock of hair that had dropped in front of his eyes. As he was talking, he would rub the tips of the fingers of his left hand together, as though contemplating something deeply important. As she stood there and watched him, it seemed that the whole world wanted to talk to him but finally after greeting the last person there and exchanging some more pleasantries, he steered her with him, towards the back of the garden.

Seats had been placed there, in a large semi-circular shape, with a podium that had been positioned at the perimeter so that everyone seated could clearly see the person at the podium.

Bethany had not noticed when all this had been arranged as she had been busy helping with setting up the catering side of things and laying out the table covers and disposable plates, cups and cutlery.

She had never ventured this far out into the garden because it backed onto woodland that had been fenced off, she assumed, so that trespassers would not enter but now she was so close, she could see that it was to stop any animals in the woodland venturing into this garden. Not that she had ever seen any animals, whilst she had been living here, but that was how it appeared.

Everyone seemed to know why they were here, as they all sat down on the seats, waiting in anticipation of what, she did not know.

Finally, the old man came up to the podium and there was a hushed silence, as everyone waited for him to speak. His voice boomed out to the audience and yet at the same time, it felt like a comforting and gentle tone that quietened and calmed everyone, to a stillness she had never experienced before. She was entranced by his tone but could not decipher the words he was speaking. It was as though he was talking a different language and yet he was not.

As time passed, different speakers took their turns to come to the front and share their messages. She had become completely engrossed in the atmosphere that had been created, so that the words they were speaking, did not matter, nor did they register with her.

Finally when the talking finished, everyone present took their seats and it was as if a silent signal had been given because suddenly, there was total silence. It lasted a full hour and, in that time, no-one fidgeted, coughed or moved. Bethany surprised herself by being able to sit still too. This was a completely new experience for her and she made a mental note to ask the old man what this was all about. She had never experienced anything like this before and it felt as though she had travelled to a different world, as time stood still.

Then, with no hint or sign, it seemed that everyone returned to their senses and started chatting and moving around. This was the signal that the "session" had drawn to an end and everyone gathered around the tables where they could pick up their plates, for the food to be served. From out of nowhere, or so it seemed to Bethany, waiters and waitresses appeared, to help serve the food and with their plates full, the crowd made their way towards the seats that they had all just vacated.

Bethany found herself automatically following the crowd, not realizing how ravenous she was and gladly accepted what was being offered to her. Without noticing, the stranger she had rescued, came to her side and guided her towards an empty table and chairs. They were both hungry and ate in silence, although observing each other at close quarters.

Once they finished, he told her to meet her by the Buddha statues, after they completed the final part of the meeting.

As everyone else finished too, they began meandering towards the woodland area, behind the garden and after passing several enormous trees, of a variety of species that Bethany recognized from her childhood, they converged around a waterfall. It seemed that the branches were bending towards each other, as though bowing in greeting by their presence and offering them shade in the midday sun, at the same time. They had traversed no more than a few hundred meters, and yet, it felt to

Bethany that they had entered a magical kingdom.
She had never explored this part of the woodland before
and was surprised to see it here.

It reminded her of her childhood, when she would often
be found wandering out in nature. She loved the smells of
the different trees, as she walked beneath their leafy
canopy, through the woodland. The oaks, ashes, aspens
and the queen of British trees, the beech, would tower
over her and she would often hug each of them in turn, in
appreciation of their magnificence. Sometimes, she
would fall asleep underneath one of them, exhausted by
her wanderlust.

She decided that when the next opportunity arose, she
would venture further afield, to investigate what other
treasures this area hid.

Once again, the crowd arrived at their allotted places
and stood in silence, allowing the sound of the waterfall
in the background, lull them into an awakened sleep.

As they stood there, deer, owls, butterflies and a range
of other wildlife slowly surfaced from their hiding places,
attracted by an unknown phenomenon.

She remembered her own similar experiences when she
was much younger and for her to witness it now, where
the animal kingdom stood beside the humans, was so awe
inspiring that she had no words for it, she was left totally
speechless. All of the animals came up close and nuzzled
their faces beside the individuals, who in turn, petted
them and spoke to them, comforting and playing with
them.

If she had not witnessed it with her own eyes, she would
never have believed it and once again, she experienced

time standing still.

Once the animals were ready, they made their way back to their hiding holes and after a brief pause, Bethany followed everyone silently, back to the house.

She had never envisaged her day would pass like this and she wanted to experience more of it.

The astounding scene she had just witnessed was like a scene out of a Disney movie and she had to pinch herself, to be certain that she had not been dreaming. Never in her wildest dreams could she have imagined this and she made a mental note to ask the old man, when she was alone with him, to make sense of this for her.

For the time being, she would let the events sit in her mind and allow her thoughts time to process what she had witnessed.

Chapter 25

As she made her way back to the house, she
remembered her assignation with the man she had
rescued and resolutely made her way towards the Buddha
statues.

There was a bench underneath the trees and she sat
herself down, awaiting the arrival of the stranger.

So many questions came bubbling to the surface that
needed to be desperately answered.

How had he survived those fatal injuries and escaped
from the two men.

What did they want from him and most important of all,
what had caused them to turn their attentions towards her
and pursue her so ferociously that it all culminated in her
losing everything. Her home, her job even her self-worth.
Her confidence, after those events had hit rock bottom,
and if it hadn`t been for the old man, she was unsure if
she could have survived the resulting chaos. Even the
security that she had carved out for herself, after
enduring so much since the untimely death of her parents
had all been shattered.

Nothing had been the same since.

At the same time, she realized, that she no longer
wished to return to that lonely monotonous life.

She had steered a new course for herself now, one that
held so much promise and magic and she did not want
those men to return and ruin what she had forged for
herself now. For so long, she had been torn between what
the outside world was saying and what she was truly

feeling inside, but now that conflict between her outer world and inner world had finally been resolved.

The old man had instilled new found behaviors and an attitude that was both inspirational and heartening and she would not let it go, without a fight. Now, finally, Bethany realized, that as long as she followed her inner heart's calling and stayed true to herself, she would be fine.

She had come to the conclusion, that she was fortunate to be living with this old couple and did not have to worry about bills or rent. Before agreeing to stay with them, she had broached the subject with the old man but he had waved her concerns away. She was working in the shop, without any recompense and in return, she would be given free accommodation. Besides, she had taken a real liking towards them and they, in turn, treated her as though she was their own daughter and gave her free rein to do as she pleased. She felt that she had been given a second chance, to redesign her life in alignment with her heart now and to make choices that would pave a future path that would bring her joy and happiness. That was not to say that there would be no challenges ahead but she was now in a much better position to deal with whatever confronted her.

As she mulled all this over, she was beginning to become impatient for answers from the stranger she had just met and doubts began to form in her mind now.

Would the stranger keep to their assignation or would he vanish again.

Just as she was about to stand up and search for him, she heard the rustle of leaves as he approached, signaling his imminent arrival.

The stranger sat down beside her and took one of her hands in his.

Bethany was taken aback by his forwardness but the words he spoke next put all that to the back of her mind.

He spoke gently and calmly.

He was her brother.

Bethany could not believe what she was hearing. What motives would her parents have for concealing this earth-shattering piece of information from her?

He had been given up for adoption, before she was born and any evidence of his existence had been erased but if she had known about it, she would have gone in search of him long ago.

He now understood why she had never come looking for him and had come to accept that they would never meet but there was a part of him that felt it was missing something.

He had been told by his parents that they had given him up for adoption because they could no longer cope with his constant disappearances. He would go missing, for several days and despite their efforts to find him, they were never successful. Several times, he had been in his bedroom but when they had summoned him, he had disappeared. At that young age, he had been vaguely aware of his ability to move in different spaces but it was only as he had got older, that he realized what he was capable of.

Bethany was confused by what he was sharing but sat in silence, allowing him to continue.

He told her that he had been given up for adoption and

this elderly couple had raised him as their own, as they had no children, educating him from home and sharing their values and ethics.

It was only after their chance meeting, when she had rescued him that he had made enquiries about her and discovered that she was his sister. He was hoping that they would meet one day but he would not instigate it, as he was unsure how he would be received.

For a moment, Bethany was completely stunned and had to take stock of what she had just been told.

Meanwhile, her brother gave her a few moments, to allow the gravity of what he had just told her, to sink in and sat in silence.

Her life was unravelling with one surprise after another but she was going with it, like a surfer caught up by a huge wave. It was both exhilarating and frightening at the same time but there was no turning back now.

The events of the day had been startling, from the gathering in the garden, the encounter with the animals and now this. Bethany had many more questions now and turned to face him, before starting.

As she sat close, observing him, she could now see how his features reminded her of their father and understood why the traits that she had witnessed earlier, reminded her of him.

Even the feeling of being a part of him, when she had rescued him made complete sense. She had wanted to lie next to him and just hold him when he had been badly hurt and somehow take away all the pain of his injuries.

It all made sense now.

The questions that had remained unanswered came out

from her mouth, all at once and she realized that what she had said made no sense at all and so she took a deep breath, calmed herself and slowly asked one question at a time.

He answered her questions slowly and patiently.

She learnt that the two men had chased him because they had discovered his secret and wanted to use his gifts to their own advantage. Initially, they had identified themselves as working on behalf of the Authorities but were not willing to elaborate what their objectives were but he had eventually discovered their true motives. They had initially disguised themselves, in order to gain his trust and after realizing their real purpose, he had disentangled himself from their clutches and finally eluded them.

He was certain, however, that at some time in the future they would be meeting again, but in the meantime, he would wait in preparation for that eventuality.

He went on to explain that from the moment he was born, he had been endowed with a gift that allowed him to travel from one dimension to another but he could not control this unique ability.

When he had been given up for adoption, the old couple had helped him to nurture his gift, until he had it under control. They were familiar with helping individuals who had been endowed with all types of special abilities at birth, and had enabled many of them to overcome their initial fears and embrace them, so that they could go out into the world to bring light into the darkest corners of the globe. At the present time, they concealed themselves, until humanity could raise and expand their vibrations, so that they could be accepted and even appreciated, for what they had to offer. He compared it to how, once upon a time, mediums and psychics were once treated with contempt and derision, because of a lack of understanding and ignorance about their abilities, and the way that witches were hounded and even burnt at the stakes.

In his case, somehow, his secret had been discovered and he had been forced to move away from the elderly couple to avoid implicating them, as he knew that his life and theirs, would be in danger.

For several years, he had managed to evade them, and when she had unwittingly come onto the scene to come to his aid, the two men must have assumed that she was associated with him and so followed her, instead, hoping that she would lead them to him.

Bethany realized now that her intuition of being watched, after meeting the stranger was correct but at the time, she had no way of understanding it all.

He had gone on to explain that when they had found him lying on the floor, unconscious, they had assumed that he would not recover from his injuries and as a precaution had rushed him to hospital, hoping he may recover. He had feigned the seriousness of his wounds in order to formulate a plan of escape and had been successful. Ever since then, he had moved from place to place, never stopping at one place, for any length of time and only ever surfacing, during these events. He was glad to be reunited with the old couple, and to finally meet her, and he would take the opportunity to spend time with her and, hopefully, find the answers that they both craved.

He would teach her all the skills he had learnt, so that she would be better equipped, should the two men return.

Bethany was certain, that there was more to what he had shared than he had told her and she was determined to get to the bottom of it.

For the moment, she was willing to accept what he had shared and make the most of being reunited with the brother she never knew existed.

Her life had dramatically changed and for the next few months she craved for some stability, before she was catapulted into the next phase. So she decided that she would take her time, to get to know him better, and more importantly, discover why his existence had been kept a secret from her.

She wondered if there was anything else that her parents had not shared with her but that was something she would never know.

So many more questions needed to be addressed but for the moment, she was grateful that she was not the sole survivor of her "clan".

She had always marveled and watched other people, as they interacted with their siblings and often wondered, what it would be like, to have a sister or a brother.

Now she had the opportunity to form that special bond and she would not put it to waste.

She walked back to the house but not before looking back, to make sure her brother was following close behind.

THE END

References

i Mark Waldman

About the author

Dina has always loved writing but only took it seriously after she left the hustle and bustle of work to begin caring for her parents.
This book has been in the making for several years and after writing biographies of her parents` life dedicated herself to completing it.
Although the work is pure fiction the events in it can be relatable to events that are current and so, hopefully, help readers to navigate a more purposeful and meaningful life.
She was inspired to publish it after prompting from a dear friend who has always encouraged and motivated her.

Printed in Great Britain
by Amazon

59979810R00129